# GRAVE CARGO

AN AIDEN MCCRAE THRILLER

E.S. HOBBS

Copyright © 2025 by Eric Hobbs

All rights reserved. No part of this book may be reproduced, stored in a retrieval system, or transmitted in any form or by any means—electronic, mechanical, photocopying, recording, or otherwise—without the prior written permission of the publisher, except in the case of brief quotations embodied in critical articles or reviews.

This is a work of fiction. Names, characters, places, organizations, and incidents either are products of the author's imagination or are used fictitiously. Any resemblance to actual persons, living or dead, events, or locales is entirely coincidental.

Cover design by L1 Graphics

First Edition

ISBN [ISBN-13]

# PROLOGUE

He wasn't a B&E man, but Aiden McCrae knew his way around a lock. The door's deadbolt was better than most, even for an overpriced McMansion.

Grade two. Brass. Four pins.

Still not a problem.

He set the tension wrench, felt the cold metal bite through his glove.

A massive A/C unit hummed next door. Sprinklers hissed over lawns. Down the block, a woman used baby talk to coax her dog along their midnight walk.

McCrae let it all fade away until there was nothing but the whisper of steel on steel.

His pick walked the pins.

One. Two. Three—

Nothing.

He eased off the pressure, shifted his angle. Tiny

tremors climbed the pick into his fingers, the lock telling its story.

There.

Pin four surrendered with a soft click. He rolled his wrist, teasing the cylinder. Another pin. Another click. Then the clean snick of the plug turning home.

The deadbolt slid back.

He eased the door open, bracing for a shrill alarm and the blast of a thousand-watt strobe.

Nothing.

At this hour, the silence was a surprise—but a relief. He could take his time now. No need to rush in blind and force this accountant to punch in a passcode.

McCrae eased into the house, gently closing the door before ghosting past a breakfast nook on his way to the kitchen. Quartz counters. Wolf stove. Under-cabinet glow. Real HGTV shit.

Photos crowded a stainless fridge—beach trips, soccer games, a man in his late thirties, and a boy who would need braces soon.

McCrae moved on. He hated when his work bled into the suburbs. Back rooms, empty warehouses, dark alleys—that's where the Commission belonged. Battles in a neighborhood like this should be fought with fountain pens, not the SIG Sauer he pulled from his jacket.

He scanned the living room, finally catching his first sign of life: a warm glow of light spilling through a doorway down the hall. He heard the soft thump of a drawer closing. The rasp of a zipper. Cartoonish voices from an upstairs TV.

McCrae twisted the suppressor onto the SIG's threaded barrel, then moved down the hall, slow and steady. He let the gun lead him into the home office.

A hard-sided suitcase gaped open on a leather sofa opposite the desk. The accountant stood near the far wall, spinning the dial on a wall safe. Rumpled dress shirt, dark-framed glasses, anxiety carved into his face.

"There," he called over his shoulder. "It's open. You want me to—"

He turned, freezing when he saw McCrae. His eyes dropped to the gun, then climbed slowly to the intruder's face.

"Not who you were expecting, huh?"

"Please," the accountant stammered. "Take whatever you want."

"We both know that's not why I'm here."

"You're with them." The man swallowed hard. "My son..."

"I won't hurt him."

"Can you do one thing? Call the police after."

McCrae had heard all kinds of last-minute bargaining through the years, but this was a first.

"My ex won't come to get him until Sunday night."

Now he understood. The accountant was worried his son would spend the weekend trapped alone with his corpse. It was admirable. He'd probably been a decent man before climbing into bed with people who weren't.

"I'll make it as easy on him as I can," McCrae said.

It was more than he should have said. Similar acts of mercy had put him at odds with the Council in the last few years. They preferred their killings loud and messy, stories written in blood as a warning to anyone who dreamed of crossing the Commission.

But McCrae still had lines he wouldn't cross.

Scarring a kid for life was among them.

His finger found the trigger. "Ready?"

"Why is this happening to me?" The accountant's voice cracked, panic surfacing unevenly. "All I did was bring some discrepancies to my boss. I've done it a million times."

McCrae's grip tightened on the SIG. Suddenly, nothing about this job felt right.

"What are you talking about?" he asked.

"I flagged pensions being paid to men with no payroll history. Showed my boss. Three days later, I'm in line for my coffee when two guys corner me claiming they're FBI."

"You don't work for the Commission?"

"*I don't know what that is!*"

This wasn't some crooked bookkeeper who flipped. This was a straight-arrow accountant who'd landed in trouble for being good at his job.

"Dad?"

Both men spun to find a small boy rubbing sleep from his eyes in the doorway. McCrae quickly shoved the SIG behind his back.

"Ethan," the accountant said, his voice soft. "Hey, buddy. It's late. Go back to bed, okay?"

The kid blinked at McCrae. "Who's that?"

"Just a friend. Here for some—"

"I'm thirsty."

His father forced a light laugh. "I'll be right up with some juice."

"The red."

"Dad knows what you like."

"You won't forget?"

"Never."

Ethan padded back toward his room, small feet whispering down the hall. A floorboard groaned from another part of the house. McCrae froze, quietly listening for a follow-up. When the silence held, he dismissed it as the growing pains of a settling house.

McCrae weighed his options. He could finish the job, walk away, pretend the accountant's story hadn't slipped past his armor. Clean. Simple. The way it was supposed to be. But the kid's face wouldn't let him go—those sleepy eyes, that oversized Sox jersey.

"Where were you headed?" he finally asked.

"What?"

"You were planning to skip town."

"Charlotte. My parents have a place there."

"Not enough. You have to disappear. Completely. Tonight. You have a passport?"

"Wait," the accountant said. "Y-you're letting me go?"

"You're still dead. From today forward. Your ex, your parents, your kid—you can never see any of them again."

"Never?"

"I promise you won't get a better deal than that."

Relief washed over the accountant hard and fast. But it vanished just as quickly.

Then his expression hardened to ice.

"That work?" he asked, lifting his voice so it carried into the hall.

McCrae's stomach sank. The accountant *had* been expecting someone else.

A smoky voice answered from behind him. "I think you missed your calling."

Jade Milano stepped into the room like she owned the place. Pressed slacks. Stiletto heels. A fitted vest over a designer blouse. It was her trademark look—boardroom chic with a body count. Milano usually carried a Laugo Alien, the 9mm's long, suppressed barrel just another sleek accessory.

Strangely, it was a Glock in her hand tonight.

"So that's it?" the accountant asked, voice thin with hope.

"That's it," Milano said. "He failed, but you passed with flying colors."

"Then I'm square?"

"All but one thing." Barely taking time to aim, Milano put a single round through the accountant's skull. Red mist spattered a bookcase with blood as the lifeless body fell, the accountant's glasses skittering across the hardwood.

McCrae lifted the SIG.

But it was too late.

A thick-necked goon stepped from the closet, his pump-action thundering.

The blast tore through McCrae's chest, folding him in half and hurling him onto his back. His head bounced off the floor. The gun flew out of his hand. Sound vanished—nothing but a high, needling drone in his ears. For a second, McCrae was sure his ribs had caved, that his lungs were on fire, that everything inside him was coming apart. Still, he clawed for the SIG, gasping for air while dragging the dead weight of his body toward his fallen weapon.

Milano's foot hovered, the stiletto heel shaped like a dagger's blade. It came down beside the SIG, snapped sideways, kicking the gun out of reach.

McCrae rolled onto his back, blinking through the blur to find Milano looming over him. She was perfectly calm when using a white cloth to wipe her pistol clean of prints. Once finished, she pressed the gun into McCrae's bloody palm.

"I'll finish up down here," she said. "You take care of the rest."

The goon's shoulders dropped. "Really?"

Milano's look was enough to erase any argument.

"Fine," he muttered. "I'm on it."

His boots thudded down the hall—then up the stairs.

Adrenaline knifed through the fog in McCrae's system. Every breath was like a shard of glass in his chest. His limbs behaved as if they belonged to someone else. He meant to beg for the boy's life, but blood rushed into his mouth and swallowed the words.

The assassin went down on one knee beside him. "Sorry, sweetheart. No one gets to pick and choose the orders they follow. Not even the great Aiden McCrae."

She kissed his forehead, then rose to her feet to stage the scene.

His vision tunneled, black clouds moving in along the edges.

Upstairs, a door creaked open.

A small voice floated down. "Dad?"

The sound of Ethan's panic ripped through McCrae with more force than the shotgun blast.

Then the darkness took him.

# ONE

*Three years later.*

After an hour directing traffic around the overturned truck, the stench had gone from bad to worse. Harris tried breathing through his mouth, but that wasn't helping. Fumes from the spill left a bitter film on his tongue and a burning in his throat.

He didn't want to imagine what this nasty shit was doing to his lungs.

"Five minutes out," Kowalski called from their cruiser.

The roll-top truck lay on its side like a gutted carcass, blocking two lanes. The crash had thrown industrial waste and debris across fifty yards of asphalt. Regular spills spread thin, followed gravity, acted like liquid. This stuff clung together in ropy strands, so thick that large chunks of waste floated on the surface like bodies in a swamp.

The driver had bolted before their arrival. They'd found his keys dangling from the ignition. Kowalski's run on the tag came back as NO RECORD FOUND. And the VIN? Gone. Nothing but scarred metal, the identifying numbers filed out of existence.

Twelve years working highway patrol. Plenty of hazmat calls.

This one felt different.

The cleanup crew finally arrived in a convoy of yellow trucks crawling through dawn's first light. Men emerged in hazmat suits. Respirators dangled from their necks until they hit the spill zone; then they were snapped into place with practiced efficiency. Within minutes, they'd transformed the accident scene into a job site, their pumps positioned with long vacuum hoses snaking toward the worst parts of the spill.

"Harris?" one of them asked when approaching.

"That's right."

"Dennis Garrett, IEPA. What's got us out here so early this morning?"

"Was hoping you could tell me," Harris said. "Looks like he lost it going around the curve. The rest is a mystery. No driver, forged manifest, one hell of a mess."

Garrett crouched near the edge of the debris field, surveying the oily rainbow coating the road. "See that discoloration? Someone mixed categories. That alone is a federal violation. Heavy metals, chromium-6, copper sulfate. And I'd bet my paycheck that's battery acid I smell."

Harris forced a laugh. "How much you make?"

There was no humor in Garrett's response. "You'll want to give us some room."

The crew was already spread out with shovels and containment drums, working systematically from the edges inward. Harris was turning to head back to the cruiser when he spotted something on the road that made his gut clench.

He shook his head as if that would scrub the image from his brain.

*Can't be*, he thought. *You're high on fumes.*

But when he looked again, it was still there—the worn heel of a work boot jutting from the slag.

Garrett barked orders at a junior member of his crew. "Tommy, watch that runoff channel. This hits a storm drain, we'll have the EPA up our ass by breakfast."

"What the—?!" Tommy's voice cracked. "Oh, fuck me!"

The kid stumbled back. His shovel dropped to the concrete. Then he tripped over his own feet and pitched backward into the waste.

Garrett moved fast for a man in protective gear. Three strides, and he had Tommy by the arm, hauling him clear of the spill. A quick inspection found no tears in the suit. Garrett's shoulders dropped in relief. "Dumbass! You realize what your mother would do to me?"

Even then, Tommy's eyes stayed locked on the slag.

Garrett followed his gaze, his body tensing up when he saw an arm floating in the soup.

There were multiple bodies in the spill.

"No! No! No!" Garrett dropped to his knees, sweeping debris aside with gloved hands.

More flesh emerged. Shredded flannel. A torso. Then a face.

Watching from beside Harris, Kowalski gagged like she was going to be sick.

The body's skin was dishwater gray, stretched drum-tight over bone. The lips were gone, leaving teeth bared in a permanent grimace. One eye brimmed with the black poison coating everything else.

Garrett cleared waste from the victim's arms, exposing the hands. Several fingers were bent at wrong angles. A closer look revealed deep ligature marks around the wrists. "What the hell am I looking at?"

"Boss!" someone shouted from nearby. "We've got a situation here!"

Garrett didn't answer.

"You hear me?"

Garrett snapped. "Would you give me a minute?!"

"Can't do it," the worker said gravely. "I need you now."

More tools clattered against the asphalt as others backed away from their positions, each of them staring into the waste as if they'd caught a glimpse into hell.

It seemed everyone was making their own horrific discovery.

Garrett lurched upright, both hands raised. "That's it! Back away! Nobody touch anything!"

One guy doubled over, retching into his mask.

Garrett spun on Harris. "I need you to call this in."

"I'm not sure who—"

"EPA has a criminal division. Tell them we've found human remains in a Class-2 spill." His words came fast, clipped. "Then Homicide. The ME—"

He stopped short, his attention shifting toward a ripple of movement in the sludge.

Garrett froze. Harris's hand found his sidearm. The world went silent.

They watched. Waited.

Then the slag shifted again.

Eyelids cracked open on one corpse to reveal orbs like clouded glass. His chest heaved in a grotesque arch. Then his mouth gaped open, sucking in a breath that was chunky and wet.

"He's alive!" Garrett shouted. "He's alive!"

Blood and foam erupted from the victim's mouth. His arms bent at impossible angles as he fought to drag himself clear of the waste. One hand broke through the surface, fingers splayed in search of something solid, something clean.

Something that wouldn't eat him alive.

Twelve years working highway patrol. Plenty of ugly crash scenes.

Harris had never seen carnage like this.

"You hearing me?" Garrett cried. "EMS! Get that bus rolling now!"

Kowalski bolted for the cruiser. "On it!"

Harris let her go. His boots felt bolted to the asphalt. He couldn't drag his eyes off the victim thrashing in the sludge. How long had this nasty shit taken to do that to a man?

More importantly, how had he been so careless? Why hadn't he grabbed one of those N95s from the trunk? This wasn't his first hazmat call. Twelve years on the job—he knew better.

And why did his face feel numb?

## TWO

Tyler Briggs greeted Castillo like he was manning the register at Lowe's, not the tool cage in the machine shop of Stateville Correctional. He'd missed the glance Castillo cut toward Krueger. Never caught the way Davis drifted into position near the grinder, eyes fixed on the guard station. The kid was too green to recognize the subtle choreography of violent men closing in on their mark.

The Feds claimed Briggs had made off with eight figures in a crypto scam before they finally tackled him in the parking lot of a Whole Foods. That should have earned him a stretch playing pickleball at some low-security camp. There he'd be just another white-collar criminal with cash waiting in the Caymans.

But in a place like Stateville?

A charge like his pinned a target on his back.

Working a few feet away, McCrae tightened his grip

on the lathe controls and forced his eyes to stay on the spinning steel. This wasn't his fight.

*You can't save everyone, man.*

The machine shop hummed with purpose all around him. The whine of a drill press. The hiss of welding torches. The echo of stock steel on metal tables. Industrial fans churned hot air thick with cutting oil and the sweat of twenty men earning thirteen cents an hour.

He eased the valve stem against the lathe's cutting tool, watching metal peel away in perfect spirals that glowed red-hot before fading out on the grease-stained floor.

"Just, uh, sign here," Briggs said.

Castillo scrawled his signature, then tossed the pen. "You're Briggs, eh?"

"Yeah. Why?"

The Dominican made a show of looking conflicted. "Ah, maybe I shouldn't say..."

Drawing closer, Krueger stopped to examine the work of another inmate with unusual interest. Davis held his position, ready to run interference when it was time.

"It's fine," Briggs said. "What's up?"

Castillo leaned in, lowering his voice. "Probably nothing. Just talk, you know? But I heard some skinheads talkin' shit. Said they got papers on you."

The kid's face drained of color. "Papers?"

"Said you got sent up on kiddie porn."

"What? No! It was nothing like that!"

Castillo raised both hands in mock surrender. "Eh, I believe you. But you know what they say about rumors. They'll get you shanked in the shower before the truth can save you."

McCrae shook his head. Not exactly Mark Twain, but close enough.

"If you want," Castillo said, "I could say something."

"R-really?"

"Not that they'll believe me. Once they hear about the shit on your hard drive."

"What?!"

Krueger had moved close enough to insert himself into the conversation. "What you really need is someone to watch your back. Lucky for you, we're in the insurance game."

"Fifty a week," Castillo said. "No one touches you."

It was the oldest play in the book: create a threat, offer protection, own the mark.

Briggs looked to the guards. Davis shifted to block his line of sight.

"They can't help you, man. Not like we can."

"You don't understand. There's nothing left. The Feds cleaned me out."

"I'm sure we'll work something out."

Krueger pushed into the cage. Briggs backed away, drill bits scattering across the concrete. Castillo was about to follow Krueger through the door when—

"Excuse me." McCrae's voice brought both inmates to

an abrupt halt. "I'm afraid there's been a misunderstanding. See—Tyler already has a policy. With me."

McCrae hadn't moved from his station. Experience had taught him that standing still was often more intimidating than charging forward.

Castillo smirked. "The fuck you say?"

"That's my client."

Castillo did some quick math. He had numbers. Krueger alone had forty pounds on McCrae. But McCrae had spent three years punishing men who mistook his lean frame and boyish features for weakness. Not to mention the rumors of his link to the men at Chicago's Westlake Hotel. Not that those things mattered now. Eyes were on them. Reputations at stake. For Castillo, backing down was no longer an option.

McCrae's own assessment was automatic. A lube sprayer was within easy reach to his right. A twenty-four-inch wrench lay on the nearest workbench. Behind him, the lathe still spun, the chuck exposed and hungry.

"I should warn you," McCrae said, "he opted for our premium protection plan."

"Man! Smash this fool!"

What happened next took eight seconds.

Davis moved first, trying to flank. McCrae snatched the lubricant gun from its hook and blasted him in the face. Davis screamed, clawing at his eyes and dropping to his knees.

Krueger charged out of the cage with a screwdriver.

But McCrae snatched a tool of his own.

The wrench moved in a violent arc he'd perfected in back alleys across the Midwest. While the setting had changed, the sound of a hyper-extended knee was exactly the same.

Krueger dropped, keening through clenched teeth.

Castillo had hoped to play clean-up; now he planned to nail McCrae while he was distracted. He lunged at him with a proper shank, filed metal wrapped in electrical tape.

McCrae slipped sideways, a step so small it barely registered with Castillo until his weight had taken him past the point of no return. McCrae caught an arm, added a twist, and let the man's momentum hurl him into the still-spinning lathe.

The chuck snagged the tail of Castillo's shirt, yanking the fabric tight. In an instant, the Dominican was locked in a tug-of-war with the machine.

"Shit! Turn it off! Turn it off!"

Castillo dropped the shank, both hands now clawing at his shirt as its fabric stretched taut across his spine, pulling him toward a cutting tool sharp enough to shave steel.

"¡Ayuda!"

This finally roused the guards.

Only they wouldn't make it in time.

He continued screaming for help, but even his allies looked away. The other inmates would watch the lathe tear Castillo to shreds before making an enemy of McCrae.

Castillo was a blubbering mess by the time McCrae slammed the emergency stop. The lathe wound down with a dying whine, but Castillo's shirt stayed cinched across his chest, every breath a chore.

McCrae leaned in for a word in private. "I don't want to talk about this again."

An alarm pierced the air.

Four guards rushed through the security gate, batons ready. McCrae set the wrench down, then laced his fingers behind his head. When they shouted for him to get down, he dropped to his knees without protest.

"McCrae, you must love spending time in the hole."

As they hauled him upright, McCrae caught Tyler Briggs staring in disbelief.

"Head down, eyes up," McCrae said. "Always leave yourself outs. Understood?"

The kid nodded.

It was all the advice McCrae could offer before they marched him away.

## THREE

Isolation broke most inmates within forty-eight hours.

McCrae was two days in and feeling pretty good.

A lonely childhood had conditioned him to find peace in solitude. He'd been an only child on a block crawling with bullies who targeted quiet kids like him. His old man was a ghost—present on paper, absent everywhere else. His mother would often vanish for days with no explanation, leaving nothing behind but an empty refrigerator and a stack of unpaid bills.

To him, the hole was just another empty apartment, another stretch of hours to fill.

It wasn't until he closed his eyes each night that he was forced to wrestle with regret—regret about choices made, regret for blood on his hands that would never wash clean.

He was finally moving past all that for the night, ready to drift off when he heard footsteps echo down the corridor. Multiple sets, unscheduled, moving with purpose.

He was already standing when a key scraped the lock, and the metal door swung open.

"Front and center, McCrae."

Two guards: Johnson and Valdez.

"Where we headed?"

Neither answered. Not the best sign. Inmates pulled from their cells in the middle of the night had a funny way of ending up in the infirmary. Sometimes the morgue.

They led him through a labyrinth of corridors before stopping at an unmarked door. After nudging McCrae forward, Johnson locked the door behind him.

Flickering fluorescents cast a web of shadows across a steel table bolted to the floor. The red light on a security camera was conspicuously dark. This was a room built to keep secrets. Apparently, Castillo wasn't waiting for McCrae's return to gen pop to get his revenge. Only it was amateur hour. The room's only door opened inward. That would leave the first man through vulnerable.

McCrae took position in the corner, poised to spring from the shadows when his target stepped into the room. Sadly, he knew he wouldn't get a crack at Castillo. The Dominican would never come through the door first. It might be Rodriguez or Lively or—

A middle-aged woman.

He'd been waiting to slam someone's face into the

hard edge of the table. Now he was the one feeling shell-shocked. He recognized her immediately, after all. How could he forget?

This was the woman who'd sentenced him to life without parole.

Black, mid-fifties, Judge Lambert wore a navy suit. Gray touched her temples, but her posture remained rigid—shoulders back, chin up. "Mr. McCrae."

"Your Honor?"

Her messenger bag hit the metal table with a dull thunk. "Mind taking a seat?"

McCrae didn't move. "If this is about the incident in the machine shop..."

Lambert looked up when his words thinned into nothing. "Yes? Go on."

He shook his head without answering. He wasn't sure where he was headed, anyway.

"Well," she continued, "you'll be happy to know Tyler Briggs has been approved for a new detail in the prison's administrative department. And I'm told life hasn't been sunshine and rainbows for Castillo, with his friends still recovering in the infirmary."

This put a grin on his face.

"Must feel nice to play the judge, jury, and executioner."

That erased it just as fast.

"What if I told you there might be a better way?"

Her hands betrayed a slight tremor when swiping the

screen on a tablet computer. He suspected fear. She couldn't be comfortable in a room alone with him. But this was fatigue. Dark circles shadowed her eyes. It was only now that McCrae noticed her blazer was a little loose through the shoulders.

McCrae filed all this away as Lambert slid her tablet across the table. She'd left it open on a photo of an overturned truck that had dumped industrial sludge across the highway.

"Three days ago, a truck carrying hazardous waste ran off the road on Route 1, just off I-94. The bodies of eight migrant workers were found in the spill."

McCrae took the tablet. He scrolled through crash pictures until he reached images of the dead. A gray hand reached out from the spill, its nails chalk-white. One victim's face was cratered with open sores, both eyes brimming with black poison.

He'd seen his share of bodies, many up close and personal. These twisted his gut.

"How long does this take?" he asked.

"You're looking at signs of extended exposure. There was a single survivor. A man named Miguel Rivera. But he won't be answering questions any time soon."

"What about the driver?"

The question slipped out before he could stop it. He still had no idea why they were meeting like this, but the professional in him couldn't help dissecting the work.

"A local man named Mike Kellner. He abandoned the scene. State police found him at home the next day. They've ruled it a suicide, but the circumstances are suspicious."

"You'd be surprised how appealing a bullet looks to people staring down the possibility of doing time in a place like this."

The judge met his eye. "You know that's not what happened here."

She wasn't wrong. One body could mean anything. But eight?

That was evidence of an operation at work.

"Manifest?"

"Fraudulent."

"What about the truck itself?"

"Unregistered, VIN removed."

"Sometimes these trucks have GPS."

"Ripped out. As of now, there's no way to track the truck's ownership or movements."

"Here's one you can answer: What does any of this have to do with me?"

"The driver was from Riveton." Lambert said this as if she'd put a flush on the table.

"Is that supposed to mean something to me?"

"A century ago, Riveton was a booming steel town. Fifty years back, the auto companies rolled in, promising steady work. Now it's just another town being crushed under the Commission's thumb."

Heat prickled beneath the scar tissue across McCrae's chest.

The Commission. His former employer.

The people who'd framed him and left him for dead.

For decades, the Commission had been little more than a group of small-time grifters, content to gnaw on scraps left behind by the bigger syndicates. But as factories closed, the Commission found opportunity where others saw ruin. While rivals continued fighting over the same blocks, the Commission staked a claim to dying towns across the Midwest.

Their business plan was simple: when good jobs moved out, the Commission moved in.

First came corner boys peddling escape by the gram. Then loan sharks, all smiles while offering interest rates that metastasized like cancer. Bookies became bar regulars, taking bets from desperate souls with nothing to lose. Soon, working girls materialized, some standing on corners across from mothers waiting to put their kids on a school bus.

And that was just the opening act.

Eventually, their work led to pictures like those on the Judge's tablet. Now, the Council ran its empire out of a collection of luxury suites high in the Westlake Hotel.

"You know," Lambert began, "there's an obscure clause in the federal code that allows a judge to recommend inmates be drafted for special assignments in times of national emergency. As luck would have it, our president has a fondness for executive orders that deem all manner of crises a national emergency. My colleagues would call my interpretation a perversion of the statute's intent."

"But?"

"They aren't here."

Silence.

"I want you to investigate the crash, see if you can find a connection to the Commission."

McCrae scoffed. "You can't be serious."

"I can arrange for a temporary release. That much will be official. The rest of our arrangement? Not so much."

"I didn't flip when I had the chance. Why would I do this?"

"You seem to be a man who can't turn a blind eye to people in harm's way."

"Because I saved one kid in the machine shop?"

"Actually, your name comes up in a lot of investigations. You pulled civilians clear of crossfire during a Toledo bank heist. Rumor has it you rescued a woman from an abusive marriage to the head of a rival family. As far as I can see, the only reason you're here—"

"I know why I'm here." His tone demanded that she not finish.

McCrae had no interest in hearing someone else argue that he was the real victim. The Commission may have framed him for a murder he didn't commit; they may have left him for dead, but that didn't make him any less guilty.

Lambert was careful with her next few words. "I was only going to say that for all the lives they've ruined, you may be more motivated to see the Commission fall than anyone. It's ironic when you think about it."

"Why's that?" McCrae asked.

"It's possible you're also the only man with the skill set needed to bring them down."

He shook his head, looking away in frustration. "This is insane."

She chuckled. "I don't disagree."

"It's also bullshit. You're a judge. If you have a case, take it to the DA."

"The DA driving a Maybach on a government salary?"

"Find someone who isn't dirty."

"Do you really trust the system to go after the Commission?"

"Don't you?!"

Sadness washed over the judge, her silence hanging between them like a confession.

"This conversation alone could cost me the robe. But this isn't the robe I dreamed of wearing. I've spent twenty-three years watching teenagers get shipped to places like this while kingpins roam free. Twenty-three years. All that time I believed…"

After hearing the waver in her voice, McCrae didn't push Lambert to finish.

"Okay," he said softly. "But I have to ask: What's the endgame?"

The judge collected herself. "I have a friend. She's an investigative journalist with a national platform. She's agreed to go public on her podcast with anything we find."

McCrae arched a single brow. "Her podcast?"

"Don't dismiss the power of a social media firestorm, Mr. McCrae. It can sway elections, bring down governments, force corporate change. If we keep feeding her stories with evidence that can't be ignored, the public may force the DA's hand, whether he likes it or not."

"Stories with an S. So this isn't a one-off. You see this as the beginning of something."

Lambert answered with a nod.

McCrae fought to get his thoughts under control. It was such an obvious setup, but he was rusty; he still couldn't see the angle. What did she stand to gain?

He searched her face for tells. She just sat there, patient but weary. Her cheeks had hollowed since he'd seen her last. She'd lost more weight than she could afford.

A shuffle echoed down the hall.

Lambert froze, her eyes darting to the door. She didn't so much as blink until the sound faded down the corridor. Only then did she let out a slow, measured breath.

It was relief. Relief that they hadn't been caught together.

This was real.

After putting him away for life, this crazy bitch was offering McCrae a second chance. Not at freedom. He'd never deserve that. But maybe a chance to do something that mattered.

And if he couldn't manage that, it was a chance to turn the monster on its creators.

That alone was one hell of a consolation prize.

"Alright," he said. "Tell me a little more about this podcast."

# FOUR

The judge had more pull than McCrae would have thought.

Three days after their midnight meeting, Lambert had him listed as part of the Scared Straight program. On paper, he'd spend most of this week visiting youth centers in the region to warn wayward kids about life inside. In reality, she'd bought him ninety-six hours to run down whatever he could on the men found in the highway spill.

When the transport officer dropped McCrae at St. Sabina's on the Southside, a car was idling in the lot, just as the judge promised. The driver didn't flinch when McCrae slid into the back. He just put the car in gear and pulled out for the long drive to Riveton.

A small messenger bag waited on the seat beside him. Inside: clean clothes; a burner phone; an Illinois driver's license—identity fake, ID flawless; an envelope thick with crisp twenties; the highway patrol's accident report and the police write-up on Mike Kellner's suicide; and, at the very bottom, a brand-new set of premium lock picks—just in case.

It was everything he'd asked for except a clean gun. Well, that and the Beau Domaine skincare products he'd requested. Instead, she'd tossed in a budget brand facial cleanser.

Disgusted, McCrae tossed the bottle out the window before turning his attention to the reports. By the time he finished reading, they were finally drifting toward an off-ramp.

"I was told you needed a lift to Riveton," the driver said. "Is there someplace in particular?"

Lambert had suggested he start with the truck—track down what he could on its history.

McCrae thought his odds were better looking into the man who'd been behind the wheel.

"You know Taylor Street?" McCrae asked.

"Sorry to say I could get you there with my eyes closed."

McCrae gave him the address listed in the report for Mike Kellner's next of kin.

For a bit, there was nothing outside but empty fields, drainage ditches, and faded billboards. Then the car slowed before turning into the first subdivision on the outskirts of town.

Once on Taylor Street, McCrae counted four houses

wearing the shame of foreclosure notices in their yards. Weeds choked driveways. Tarps stretched across roofs. A neighborhood park had fallen into disrepair, the swings from its swing set missing.

When the driver pulled to the curb, McCrae thanked him and slid out of the car.

His boots felt heavy climbing the porch steps. Ringing the bell brought a woman's cough to life, followed by the sound of a chain sliding back and two deadbolts being disengaged.

The old woman answered in an oversized flannel, fuzzy slippers, and nothing else.

"Mrs. Kellner?"

Deep lines cut brackets around her scowling mouth. She kept a cigarette pack visible in her breast pocket like a badge of defiance against doctors' orders and common sense.

"That depends," she said. "Who's asking?"

"My name's Alan. I was a friend of Mike's from back in the day."

"Is that right?" she asked skeptically.

"I hope I'm not bothering you. I know you've been through a lot. I would have made the viewing, but I didn't hear what happened until—"

"Total shit show."

"I'm sorry?"

Her words came fast and bitter. "Everyone muttering lies about my boy behind my back like I can't hear 'em.

You know it isn't true, right? What they're saying? Michael had nothing to do with them Mexicans."

McCrae kept his voice level. "Anyone who knew him knows that."

"Well, get in here. I'm on a fixed income. Can't pay to keep the whole block cool."

He wasn't surprised by the memorial waiting in her living room.

Photos of Mike Kellner crowded mantels and end tables. Smiling a gap-toothed grin at six. Kneeling in shoulder pads with a helmet tucked under his arm. Posed for pictures with his date for the prom. The newest had Mike leaning against the chrome grill of a semi-truck.

McCrae had seen enough men die young to know this story well. These weren't photos that had accumulated over years of living. This was a shrine assembled in haste.

Already tapping out a cigarette, Mrs. Kellner collapsed into a well-worn recliner. "So how did you know Michael?"

McCrae sat on the sofa. "It's hard to remember how we met. We ran in similar friend groups. He was the one who helped me get my CDL license."

"You're a trucker?"

"For a few years. I couldn't handle the hours."

A proud smile lifted her face. "Michael loved the road. Bought a truck of his own so he could work as an independent contractor." She said this as if he'd spent his days curing cancer.

"Is that the truck he was driving on the night of the crash?"

She shook her head. "He had to sell the semi a few months back. Said the maintenance costs didn't make sense. He had a mind for that kind of thing. He was always working but never punched a clock a day in his life. He was—what do you call it—an entrepreneur."

McCrae picked up the framed photo of Mike with his truck. He wore the kind of smile saved for the biggest events in life, but there was also a hint of panic in his eyes, as if he already knew he'd bitten off more than he could chew.

"If he'd been born anywhere but Riveton. His father always promised to get us out, but..." There was no need to finish such a familiar story.

"Mrs. Kellner, do you know anything about the people who hired him for this last job?"

"Now why does everyone keep asking that?" she snapped.

"Like who?"

An oven timer chimed from the kitchen before she could answer.

"Hold that thought."

When she left, McCrae stood to take a lap around the room.

White doilies protected hand-me-down furniture. She owned an impressive collection of sterling silverware, but there were bullet holes in the display case, gaps where pieces had been removed. It was either the slow bleed of poverty or a sign of unexpected money problems. Maybe the same issues that had forced her son to sell his prized semi.

The front door pushed open without warning. "Ma? You home? I—"

The Kellner boy froze in the doorway. Mid-thirties, construction-worker build, steel-toed boots still dusty from a job site. "Who the hell are you?"

"No one to worry about," McCrae said. "Just a friend of Mike's stopping to pay my respects."

"These last few years, Mike didn't have no friends. Why don't you try again?"

McCrae could already see he was going to get more out of Mike's brother than his mother.

"Who sent you? Torrino? Colfax? One of them?"

Mrs. Kellner called out from the kitchen. "Bryce, is that you?"

He took a step toward McCrae, continuing in a low voice so his mother wouldn't hear. "Whatever business you had with Mike is done. You come around looking to get something out of her, you're going to find out real quick you aren't the only ones in Riveton with guns."

His hand found the handle of a work knife clipped to his belt. He pulled it like he meant to put in some overtime.

McCrae put both hands in the air. "What are you doing, man?"

"This is me asking you to leave."

Bryce was certainly playing the part, but that's just what it was—an act.

"You hungry?" Mrs. Kellner asked, completely oblivious to the growing tension in her front room. "Tammy Duckworth brought enough casserole to feed half the state." She lowered her voice for the rest. "Woman wears more makeup than a Vegas whore."

Bryce's attention shifted to the kitchen doorway.

That was all the opening McCrae needed.

His left hand clamped onto Bryce's wrist. His right slid to the elbow, turning the joint into a lever. One sharp twist folded Bryce. The knife fell to the carpet as a groan tore from Bryce's throat.

"Answer your mother."

Bryce tested the hold. Got nowhere. He threw a wild shot with his free hand—a desperate haymaker with no chance of landing.

McCrae drove the captured arm down and back. Leverage did the rest. Tendons screamed as Bryce's shoulder buckled and his hand was forced up between his shoulder blades.

"If she finds us going at it, you'll have more explaining to do than me."

The fight finally drained out of Bryce. "Whatever! Okay! Just get off me!"

McCrae released him, stepping back but staying ready. "Tell her we're going to step outside."

"Ma, me and... this guy... we're gonna grab a smoke."

"What about dinner?"

Bryce shook his head, smirked. "Tammy's casserole is fine."

"We'll see about that," Mrs. Kellner muttered to herself.

The backyard held a rusted Weber grill standing guard over a weathered picnic table, its boards splintering away. Along the property line, an entire section of the fence was missing.

Bryce fished a pack of Marlboros from his pocket. His hand shook as he thumbed the lighter to life. McCrae let him have the silence, gave him room to steady himself on a long drag.

"Well," Bryce said at last, throwing his arms wide, "talk."

"What happened to Mike?"

"They don't have the internet where you're from?"

McCrae waited for Bryce's tough-guy posture to collapse under its own weight.

"He was dead the second he borrowed that money," Bryce said.

"How much?"

The answer came in a cloud of smoke. "Twenty grand. Interest ran it to thirty. Forty came faster. When he fell behind a few weeks, they worked him over real bad. Couple days later, they told him they knew a way he could work off his debt."

"Driving the truck."

"Midnight runs."

"Hauling what?" McCrae asked.

Bryce answered with a humorless laugh. "Toxic waste and dead Mexicans."

"Did he know that's what he was carrying?"

"He knew about the waste. They had him hauling it somewhere across the state line. I don't think he knew anything about the bodies."

His story sounded reasonable enough. Waste management had always been an industry ripe for exploitation by outfits like the Commission.

Bryce nodded toward the house. "She talks about him like he was the Second Coming. The only time she saw his face was on the first when her check came in."

"What about the pickups?" McCrae asked. "You know anything about those?"

Bryce shook his head.

"Is there a place in town you think a deal like that is more likely to go down? A bar where drivers hang out when they come in off the road?"

"The Blue Note? It's not a bar, but I went to school with a kid who got busted selling crystal to drivers in the lot."

McCrae showed his appreciation with a nod.

"How'd I let this happen?" Bryce asked, his voice sounding weary. "He was my little brother, man. And I knew. I fucking knew where this was heading."

"There's nothing you could have done."

"How do you know?"

McCrae didn't answer. What was he going to say? That he knew because Mike Kellner was just one more body produced by a machine that he helped build?

"I'm going to be in town a few days, staying at the Eastside Motel." Bryce's eyes flicked up at the name, his cigarette pausing halfway to his lips. "If you run into any problems—guys looking for money, making threats—you come find me. We'll see what we can do."

McCrae started toward the gap in the fence so he could leave without facing Mrs. Kellner.

Bryce called after him. "The fuck do you care what happens to us?"

McCrae answered over his shoulder. "Mike wasn't the only one with a debt to pay."

# FIVE

There was a pretty young thing turning tricks in an RV permanently parked behind the Blue Note Diner. That's how McCrae knew he was in the right place.

He'd gotten all he was going to get from the Kellners—a grieving mother's denial and a brother's bitter truths. But midnight runs like the ones Bryce described didn't organize themselves. Someone had recruited Mike Kellner, pointed him toward that truck, and counted on desperation to keep him quiet.

Bryce was right to think deals like that were likely to originate here.

A mile down from the Route 1 junction with I-94, the Blue Note was a throwback diner that had somehow survived the onslaught of corporate chains. Fluorescent tubes threw harsh light across cracked vinyl booths and chipped countertops. It was noisy with conversation, the clatter of plates, and the occasional hiss of air brakes from the lot outside.

McCrae chose a corner booth, with his back to the wall so he had clear angles on both exits and the parking lot. A curved mirror over the register provided a view around the corner.

He'd only been sitting for a minute when a waitress appeared beside the table. Late twenties, dark hair pulled back. She had a beauty that was likely to boost her tips with some while inviting unwanted advances from others. A button pinned to her apron read KNOW YOUR RIGHTS in English and Spanish. Beneath that, her name tag read ROSA.

"Know what you want?" she asked. "Or are you gonna need a little more time?"

The laminated menu felt awkward in his hands. Inside, you ate what was dumped on your tray—usually gray protein alongside wilted vegetables and bread that could double as a weapon. Here, he had so many choices he wasn't sure where to start.

"Still deciding," he said.

"The meatloaf's pretty good. It's what most these guys go for on Tuesday."

"That works."

When she left, McCrae continued taking stock of the room. Three truckers sat hunched over the counter, chewing over politics. Two more in a back booth kept their voices low, one sliding an envelope under the table.

By the window, a glassy-eyed driver checked his phone every ten seconds, his leg jackhammering with the frantic energy of a man high on pills.

That was his man—wired, alone, a guy desperate for someone to listen.

McCrae stayed put. No sense spooking him. Better to let the kid finish up, pay his tab, and drift out to the lot. Out there, a little respect would go a long way. That, and some empathy.

Then the kid would spill everything he knew and walk away thinking it had been his idea.

Rosa returned with his plate. The meatloaf looked better than anything he'd eaten in three years. Steam rose from real mashed potatoes. The green beans were actually green.

"Look good?" she asked.

"You have no idea."

Certain the rich food would hit his gut hard, McCrae took his time. Besides, who knew when he would have an opportunity to eat like this again?

Local news played on a wall-mounted TV behind the counter. He caught fragments from a few stories, but nothing was interesting enough to pull him away from his plate.

Not until they offered an update on the recent highway spill.

After a few comments from law enforcement, they cut

to an interview with a real estate developer named Dean Holbrook.

On his way to the Blue Note, McCrae had seen signs around town. Green. Gold. Pristine.

**RIVETON WILL RISE**
**Holbrook Properties**

Now he had a face to put with the name. Early thirties. Gelled hair. Clean-shaven. He wore an expensive button-up with the sleeves rolled to his elbows. The uniform of a polished politician who wanted to portray himself as a friend to the working man.

"These tragic deaths underscore a larger problem in Riveton," Holbrook said. His voice carried the right mix of concern and authority. "Criminal elements are drawn to these abandoned communities. Empty buildings morph into drug dens. Vacant lots become dumping grounds. This is exactly why the waterfront project is so important to our city."

The reporter pressed him before he could get too carried away with his talking points. "And how do you respond to those who suggest the truck may have originated from the waterfront?"

"That we need to let all the facts come in before we start assigning blame. Yes, the waste found in the spill is similar in makeup to the contamination we're currently removing from the foundry site. But there are similar cleanups happening throughout the state. This truck could have come from any of them. In the meantime, we're cooperating fully with the investigation. After all, the waterfront revitalization won't be enough on its own. It's only after we drive out these undesirable elements that we can begin attracting the business and economic investments needed to ensure Riveton will rise again."

The broadcast cut back to the studio, but the segment had run long enough for McCrae to get a read on Holbrook. This was a man who'd hunt down a camera to spin any story in his favor. He'd even managed to squeeze in his tagline at the end.

At the counter, a guy in a beat-to-hell Carhartt snorted at the TV. "I thought he was nothin' more than a college puke when he came in here that time to kiss babies and shake hands."

"More like kiss ass and shake us down," someone said from a nearby table.

"But he's got a point," the Carhartt continued. "Clean up the neighborhoods, crime goes away. Not to mention the illegals on every corner."

Listening from a spot three stools down, Rosa attacked an already clean stretch of counter, her rag working in short, violent strokes.

Someone else chimed in. "Junior's just covering his own ass."

"How you figure?"

"You know that truck came out of the old foundry."

"Even if it did—that don't make him responsible for the bodies."

"He had to know something."

"Bullshit! Some MS-13ers dumped those bodies when no one was looking. Or am I the only one who noticed every one of them was a Mexi-can't?"

Rosa looked up sharply. "Mexi-what?"

The mouthy guy shut down like she'd yanked his plug.

"I knew most of those men. You're more likely to be Mara Salvatrucha."

"And what's that?"

"Exactly! You don't even know what you're talking about."

"Look. I'm sorry. I know you're one of the good ones. But—"

"The good ones?"

"Yeah."

Rosa dug a pad from her apron, scribbled something furiously, then smacked a receipt down on the counter. "They'll take you at the register."

"Jesus! Learn to take a compliment."

"Sure..."

"What if I want some pie?"

Rosa was already marching onto the serving floor. "I wish I could help you, but we're so busy, I'm afraid I just *can't*."

Just like that, the show was over.

McCrae checked on the pillhead before using a roll to soak up some gravy. He was just finishing his meal when Rosa stopped again.

"You good?" she asked.

"Rough night?"

She looked up, confusion creasing her brow. "I'm sorry?"

He tilted his head toward the counter crowd. "Assholes are always the loudest."

She blew out a tired sigh. "Right."

"You say you knew those men?"

She nodded, her lips pressed tightly together against the grief welling up inside her.

"Have the families gotten an update on what may have happened?"

"They've made it clear we won't be getting an update."

"What do you mean?"

She studied McCrae as if trying to decide if he was someone she could trust.

"I've heard the truck's manifest was a fake," he said.

She slid into the booth across from him. "It runs deeper than that. Every one of those men they found was taken out of the Home Depot parking lot by ICE."

McCrae wasn't sure he'd heard her right. "You're kidding?"

"No warrant, no badges. Just masked men in plain clothes snatching people off the street. They wouldn't even tell us where they were taken. Now we know why."

"Were those men the only ones taken?"

"Twenty-two in all. That leaves fourteen unaccounted for."

Something outside finally pulled the twitchy kid by the window to his feet. He hustled through the door, the bell ringing as he slipped into the night.

McCrae let him go.

He couldn't believe the government was responsible for the murder and disposal of those men found in the spill. But he also had to make sure he wasn't out here chasing a connection to the Commission that didn't exist. That meant chasing down every lead. Besides, there was value in knowing the victims. They'd probably tell him more than digging into the driver's life ever could.

"Have the families considered hiring an immigration attorney?"

"You're looking at the best they can afford."

"Well, maybe I can help."

"Do you know people in Homeland Security?" Rosa asked excitedly.

"No."

Rosa slumped back in her seat. "Oh..."

"But I do have experience asking questions in a way that makes them impossible to ignore."

She straightened up again, suspicion returning to

harden her features. "Dude, I'm not going to sleep with you."

He choked back laughter. "I'm sorry?"

"If this is some backwards way to hit on me…"

He laughed harder. "I promise, it's not. No, I knew Mike Kellner."

"The driver?"

McCrae nodded. "I think we both want to know who put him behind the wheel of that truck. Maybe we can help each other."

Rosa drew back, her eyes narrowing as she sized him up one last time. She eventually rose from the booth and smoothed her apron. "I didn't catch your name."

His thoughts flashed to the fake license in his wallet with the name Alan Brooks. "McCrae."

She smirked. "What did your mama call you?"

His mind flipped through a list of his mother's favorites—soft, lazy, pathetic. She had a gift for turning simple words into weapons. She loved to remind him his birth was a mistake and often joked she hoped to die young so she wasn't around to watch him "go fag."

"Aiden," he finally said.

"Okay, Aiden. Tomorrow. Out front. 8 a.m."

"And just to be clear," McCrae said with a mischievous grin, "this isn't a date?"

A smile brightened her face, the first he'd seen from her all night. "You need anything else?"

"Just the bill."

Rosa shook her head. "It's on the house."

# SIX

The Eastside Motel was laid out beside the road like it had lost a fight. Several letters in the neon sign had given up long ago, leaving a Hangman board to flicker against the night. Working girls chain-smoked cigarettes near a busted ice machine. A dealer worked the corner, hoodie up despite the heat. Two drunks shared a bottle wrapped in brown paper.

An Asian woman waited behind bulletproof glass, her acrylic nails tapping away at the shattered screen of a dated Samsung. When McCrae pushed into the lobby, she didn't look up to greet him.

"Twenty an hour, forty-five for the night. Cash only, paid up front."

"I need a room through Sunday," McCrae said. "End unit, if you've got it." He slid a stack through the slot.

Finally looking up, she eyed the crisp bills as if they changed everything.

"Just you?" she asked, a wicked smile suggesting this was a problem she could easily fix.

He nodded.

She rose to better showcase her ripped fishnets. "Need company?"

"Just the room."

Her flirty smile died fast. She slid a key through the slot, then dropped back onto her stool, those acrylic talons resuming their assault on the cracked screen.

"Room twelve," she muttered.

Outside, the open-air corridor ran past a row of doors, each hiding someone who'd failed to outrun their demons.

Room three leaked the stink of burning plastic. Meth, maybe crack. Either way, someone was destroying themselves one hit at a time.

From eight came manic laughter that collapsed into a raw, heartbroken sob.

In ten, the curtains swayed, a pale face flashing between them before vanishing into the dark.

His own door opened onto piss-yellow carpet with paths worn down to the foundation. Ceiling stains mapped rust-belt decay. Anything of value was bolted down. The AC worked, and the sheets were clean, but both were a close call.

McCrae shook his head in disbelief.

Or was it shame?

What a stupid kid he'd been. How many nights had he spent feeling proud that his work required him to hole up in similar shitholes? Back when he was first running with the Commission, when he was sure he'd finally found a place he belonged.

Before the betrayal.

Before his sins became so great he couldn't be redeemed.

He locked the door. Tested it. Slid the deadbolt. Tested again.

A crack in the bathroom mirror sliced his reflection in two. A narrow window would be big enough, in a pinch, for a man who'd learned to make himself small.

The shower kicked on hot with decent pressure, but the water stank of rotten eggs. He stayed under just long enough to strip the sweat from his body and the oil from his face.

He spent twenty minutes watching through the blinds before finally accepting he was safe.

A flyer waited on the nightstand. It offered a rendering of Holbrook's vision for the city's waterfront. Kids splashed in computer-generated fountains. Couples pushed strollers past boutiques. A happy couple enjoyed the view from a condo balcony. Down the side, a neat column of bullet points promised JOBS, SAFETY, and GROWTH under the same tagline he'd seen plastered all over town: RIVETON WILL RISE.

Whoever he was, this Holbrook was putting on a full-court press.

McCrae tried the TV but found himself faced with too many choices: fifty channels of nothing, Netflix. After thumbing around for half an hour, he finally clicked it off and climbed into bed.

It should have been a luxury.

It felt more like quicksand.

The mattress gave under his weight, the softness threatening to swallow him.

He tried lying on his side. His back. Legs straight, legs bent, a pillow between his knees.

When he finally thought he'd found some comfort, McCrae realized he couldn't hear much over the AC's rattle. In prison, he heard it all, knew what sounds to be wary of. Here, he was blind.

Two hours passed, and he was no closer to sleep. His jaw was clenched, his muscles tight.

Had three years really been enough to make him into an institutionalized man?

He finally gave up.

McCrae rolled out of bed, shut off the AC, and cracked a window. Heat crept in, but with it came clarity: traffic, music from a parked car, an argument on the corner, a woman moaning "Daddy" from two doors down.

He was disgusted to discover he already felt more at ease.

McCrae grabbed his pillow and a sheet, then set up

on the floor. Finally comfortable, he ran through the details of his first day: Mike Kellner, crushed by debt until hauling illegal loads felt like the only way out; Rosa's story about ICE snatching migrants off the street, all of them missing until eight turned up half-dissolved in the toxic spill from Kellner's truck. He saw no obvious connection between the stories, but tomorrow would give him more to work with. Rosa was convinced ICE would stonewall him the same way they had everyone else. McCrae knew better. Rooms like this had taught him that everyone broke, eventually.

The only question was how much pressure it would take.

## SEVEN

McCrae worried that this little errand with the waitress would take all day.

Rush hour tacked an extra forty-five minutes onto their trip, turning their quick city run into a crawl before the Chicago skyline even appeared on the horizon. Now, even if they got in and out quickly, they wouldn't roll back into Riveton until well after lunch.

From the looks of things, even that was wishful thinking.

ICE kept a field office one block south of the Dirksen Building downtown. Its waiting room felt more like a holding pen. Plastic chairs were bolted down in long rows, forcing strangers to sit thigh to thigh and shoulder to shoulder.

A housekeeper sobbed into a wad of paper napkins. A man in paint-splattered boots perched on the edge of his seat, his callused hands trembling. Parents fought a losing battle with restless kids who'd been told to sit still for too long. Most clung to personal documents as if they were the only thing preventing them from sinking through the floor.

When numbers were called, the owner often rose with the slow walk of the condemned. They'd come for help, but everyone knew it could just as easily go the other way. ICE could pull them from the brink—or shove them over the edge. And there was no way of knowing what would happen until they were behind closed doors.

McCrae and Rosa had been crammed into those awful chairs for two hours by the time their number was finally called.

An assistant waited for them near the room's side door. "Mr. Heller will see you now."

The office was everything McCrae expected: an American flag in the corner, procedural posters on proper documentation, and a portrait of the president glaring down from the wall.

Heller looked up from behind his desk. Early forties. Male pattern baldness. A blazer way too small across his gut. It was easy to imagine him hacking his way around some shitty municipal golf course on weekends.

"Ms. Delgado," he said. "Back again, I see."

Rosa took a seat. "Did you think I would become less persistent after last week?"

"You've already lost me."

"The bodies found in the highway spill? Surely you recognized their names. I've probably mentioned every one of them at some point."

"I suppose that's the one benefit of an open border policy. Sometimes illegals take each other out so American taxpayers aren't stuck footing the bill."

Heller smirked as if he was proud of that one.

Ignoring the dig meant to rattle her, Rosa arranged papers in a row along the edge of his desk. "These men were apprehended by your agents at the same time and place as those found buried in the waste. I'm not leaving until I know exactly where they're being held."

"As I've already explained multiple times, our website contains all the publicly available information on detainees."

"I've spent hours on your website. Nothing comes up when I search their names."

"Then they're not in our system."

"Obviously!"

"Which means they weren't taken."

Rosa opened the Notes app on her phone. "Would you like me to run you through a list of the broken links I've found on your website? At last count, there were fifty-six that pointed to pages that don't exist."

"But the database is fully functional. If you have the proper information for a detainee—name, DOB, country of origin—you'll have no problem finding them."

"Unless you used an abbreviation for the country. Or

forgot to hyphenate a name. Or used a different format for the date of birth. My search has to match your entry exactly, or I get an error message."

"Have you considered these men may have moved on? Who knows? Maybe they decided to self-deport so they could get in line like they should have done from the very start."

Rosa was ready for this, too. She swiped through her photos, pulled up a video, then angled the phone so Heller could see the security cam footage saved to the device.

McCrae leaned in for a better look. On screen, a crowd of Hispanic men stood clustered near the contractor entrance of a Home Depot.

Then the cargo vans rolled in.

"Where did you get this?" Heller asked, his voice tightening.

She didn't answer.

Masked agents in tactical gear spilled from the windowless vehicles. They moved through the crowd with precision, rifles low but ready. Each takedown was a masterclass in efficiency, pressure points exploited, joints locked. Running immigrants triggered flanking maneuvers executed by men who'd clearly seen action in combat zones.

This was far different from the viral videos McCrae had seen online—ICE agents stumbling over each other like police academy rejects, all aggression and no training.

He felt like Seal Team 6 had been dropped on the wrong side of the map.

Heller shook his head after watching two agents shove one man's face into the concrete. "They always make it so hard on themselves. Someone should tell your people that a little cooperation would go a long way."

"They're supposed to cooperate with armed men in masks who just attack them out of nowhere?"

"And how do I know these arrests are connected to the men on your list?"

"Why else would I be here?" Rosa asked sharply.

"I've been asking myself that same question for two months. Now, if you'll excuse me, between overly dramatic wives sobbing their eyes out and the bleeding-heart lawyers working pro bono, there are a lot more people waiting to yell at me today."

Rosa groaned, hanging her head in defeat.

But McCrae wasn't ready to give up. "Maybe we can put this behind us if you give her a quick look at the comprehensive list of detainees."

Heller looked over as if he were seeing McCrae for the first time. "Who are you again?"

"I'm here for emotional support."

"Well, if I did that for her, everyone would expect the same."

"What happened to the guy lecturing her on cooperation?"

"Even if I could, I can't."

"You won't."

Heller rose from his seat, shoulders lifting in an exasperated shrug. "Is there a difference?"

"Sure." McCrae's tone made it clear he thought this was a stupid question. "Can't is set in stone. Won't is movable. You just have to find the right buttons to push."

"Good luck with that." Heller rounded the desk as if he was planning to walk them out. "It was a pleasure as always, Ms. Delgado."

He offered his hand, but she just frowned before starting toward the door.

McCrae was more open to accepting the polite gesture. He took Heller's hand, his grip snapping shut like a trap. He found the narrow groove between Heller's thumb and forefinger, applying pressure to the nerve bundle until it caught fire.

Heller's breath hitched—surprise first, then pain. The confident smirk vanished.

"Buttons are everywhere, right? This one's called the radial nerve. It'll wake you up in the morning, but I'm not sure it's enough to change minds. Let's see what else we can find."

Rosa spun just in time to see McCrae's hand snap up, fingers clamping down on the soft notch at the base of Heller's neck.

Heller's knees buckled. His eyes rolled back. His mouth gaped in a silent scream.

"I think we have a winner!"

"What the hell are you doing?!" Rosa shouted.

Ignoring her, McCrae maintained the hold while steering Heller back to his chair. Years of practice had taught him the perfect amount of pressure—enough to avoid serious injury, plenty to reset the pecking order in any room.

"Nobody's asking you to be a hero," McCrae said. "Just do your job."

Heller tried twisting away from McCrae's vice-like grip. "Do you have any idea the trouble you're in? I'm a federal officer. You can't just—"

A shot to the solar plexus dropped him back into his chair. He gasped for air.

"Aiden! Enough! You're taking this too far!"

McCrae turned toward her. "Give me a name. Someone found in the spill."

She couldn't peel her attention from Heller.

"He'll be fine, Rosa. He just needs a minute to catch his breath."

She squeezed her eyes shut, as if that alone would make this go away. "P-Paul Esperanza."

McCrae released the hold but stayed close. "Filter the database so we're only looking at the people taken from Riveton."

Seeming to shrink before their eyes, Heller brought trembling hands to the keyboard.

Just as McCrae suspected, he was easily able to extract the names of migrants who'd been taken in Rosa's town. Over three hundred had been taken into custody this year alone.

"Scroll to the names that start with E."

Heller obeyed but found no one listed with the name Esperanza.

"Who else?" McCrae asked.

"Javier Morales," Rosa said.

The database spit back plenty of men named Morales, but not a single Javier.

Two more searches yielded the same result—nothing. None of the men buried in that roll-top truck were in the ICE database.

"They deleted them," Rosa said. "It's the only thing that makes sense."

Heller shook his head but stayed quiet.

McCrae said, "Give me someone who wasn't taken from the Home Depot."

Rosa shuffled through her papers. "Gloria Rodriguez."

This time, the name was there. Every detail on Gloria Rodriguez was available. Alien registration number. Country of birth. Custody status. Even the name and address of the detention facility where she was being held. Everything was listed just as it should be.

"We're done," McCrae said.

"What happened?" Rosa asked breathlessly. "Did she come up?"

"She's being held in Chippewa County."

"Where's that?"

"Michigan."

Heller slumped in his chair as they started for the door. McCrae had finished with him, but the moron's pride wouldn't let them go without lashing out. "We're always the bad guy until someone's kicking down your door. Then who you gonna call?"

McCrae couldn't resist one last shot. "I've known a lot of crooked cops in my day."

"I'm sure you have."

"Never met any so dirty they had to 'protect and serve' from behind a mask."

Anger snapped Heller to his feet. "Our people get death threats. Their families live in fear. You people can't wait to ruin the life of an agent doing his job!"

McCrae pulled the door shut behind them. Heller continued hollering from the other side, but they didn't have time for a debate. For all the hours they'd burned on their trip to the city, McCrae walked away having learned just one thing.

The men taken in the Home Depot raid—including those found in the highway spill—did not exist in the ICE database.

Now he had to find out why.

# EIGHT

Rosa's pickup rattled away from the Federal Building, the weak AC losing its battle against Midwest humidity. A rosary swayed from the rearview mirror. Family photos were tucked into the sun visor—Rosa smiling alongside the people she was fighting so hard to protect.

Only there was no smile today. "What the hell were you thinking?"

McCrae stayed quiet, eyes fixed on the window.

The transmission protested loudly as they accelerated onto the freeway.

"I'm not you, okay? I'm not here for one friend. I'm here for every family in the barrio. I have to keep the lines of communication open."

"You're right," McCrae said. "I'm sorry."

The elevated freeway cut a gray path over crumbling

row houses. Commercial buildings sagged under layers of graffiti. Junkies drifted like ghosts across train platforms, chasing whatever fix got them through the day.

"Where'd you learn to do that?" Rosa finally asked. "The pressure point thing?"

McCrae shrugged. "Internet."

"Bullshit." The edge in her voice got his attention. "You handled him like you're from one of those movies."

"What movies?"

"You know what I'm talking about. *John Wick. The Equalizer.* That shit."

He laughed.

"Seriously, I wanna know who I've got in my truck."

A burned-out apartment building slid past. Most of the windows were boarded up, but two were left bare so they looked like empty eye sockets watching everyone that went by.

"I was small for my age. Grew up in a bad neighborhood. I couldn't fight my way out of a wet paper bag, so I had two choices: find intelligent ways to defend myself or learn to enjoy getting my ass kicked."

"So you really learned all that on YouTube?"

"I got my start online, but trying to use what I saw in those videos only made things worse. I had to find someone who would help me implement the techniques I'd been studying."

"And how old were you?"

"Twelve."

"So this guy just taught that stuff to some random sixth grader off the street?"

McCrae shifted back to the window. "It took some convincing."

"I bet no one messed with you after that."

"I did develop a reputation. Only..." His response trailed off.

"Yeah?"

He shook his head as if there was nothing more to the story.

But there was. More than he cared to share.

When word of his newfound skills had reached the Commission, they'd treated him like some kind of street-level prodigy. They couldn't wait to bring him into the fold.

Learning to defend himself had been the first step toward a life that cost him everything.

Through the window, the city gave way to abandoned smokestacks against the gray sky. The city was long behind them when Rosa finally broke the silence again.

"In Guatemala, my parents were journalists. Well—activists. They ran social media accounts that tracked cartel activity, reported cops on the take, fingered corrupt politicians. They tried to cover their tracks, but they were more concerned with exposing the truth, you know?"

McCrae already sensed this story would have an ending not unlike his own.

"I was eight when they came." Her voice stayed steady,

but her hands tightened on the wheel. "They had badges, but they were police in name only."

She used the Riveton exit as an excuse to keep her attention locked on the road. McCrae waited, letting her choose whether to continue.

"My father had just enough time to stash me in the closet, but I... I was able to watch what happened through the slats. Light from the window turned them into... silhouettes. It felt like a bad dream. Like shadow men had come alive to attack my dad. Stupid, right?"

"Not for a girl that age."

"My mother found me after. We caught the first bus north and never looked back."

McCrae pictured her childhood trek across a punishing landscape—deserts, rivers, endless miles of scrub. He saw her tiny body crouched in the shadows of a freight yard, her small hand welded to her mother's while coyotes argued over payment. He saw her trembling under a truck bed tarp while gunfire cracked somewhere in the distance. The reel of imagined moments ran just long enough that McCrae missed Rosa turning into an aging neighborhood just off Riveton's square.

Graffiti had given way to full-blown murals celebrating Central American culture. Kids owned the street, their shouts bouncing off parked cars as parents watched from porches. A Bears jersey streaked past. Scuffed Jordans skidded through a chalk line. Flags drooped from second-story windows. Guatemalan blues, Salvadoran whites, Mexican green. Some were stitched to the Stars and Stripes. Heritage and patriotism, side by side.

"Rosa, where are we going?"

She pulled to the curb at an old house where half the neighborhood seemed to be congregating in the front yard. "Hope you brought your appetite."

His chest tightened. Through the front window, kids were setting a table; a woman was stirring a big pot on the stove. It was a normal family doing normal things.

"I can't do this," he muttered.

Rosa squeezed his hand. "I won't let anything happen to you."

She was about to climb from behind the wheel when he grabbed her wrist—gripped it much harder than he intended. "I'm not the man you bring home to Mom."

Her expression shifted—surprise first, then a tightening that looked like worry. "What are you talking about?"

He pictured her at eight years old, small and terrified in that closet, watching those shadow men go to work on her father. How would she look at McCrae if she knew he'd orphaned his fair share of kids?

He finally loosened his grip, allowing Rosa's hand to fall away. "Nothing."

Outside, a pear-shaped woman stepped onto the porch. She had Rosa's face, only her features were carved deeper by years of worry. It was only when Rosa climbed from the truck that those lines softened in the warmth of a mother's love, an emotion as unfiltered and genuine as the panic now clawing its way up McCrae's throat.

# NINE

Several teenage boys were already moving to intercept McCrae as he exited the truck. They did their best to look tough, but McCrae could read potential violence in a glance. Not one of these kids was a genuine threat, and none was tougher than his host.

Rosa quickly cut them off. "¡Para! Está bien. He's with me."

One kid, maybe nineteen, continued glaring as if he wouldn't be satisfied until the uninvited white boy was gone from his neighborhood. McCrae couldn't wait to oblige.

This was as far from the comfort of solitary confinement as one could get.

He followed Rosa through the gate, dodging a swarm of kids playing soccer in the yard. Some spoke Spanish. Others English. Most were shouting in a mix of both, switching back and forth between the languages mid-sentence like it was nothing.

Rosa climbed the steps, then kissed her mother's cheek before turning toward McCrae. "Mama, this is the man I told you about. Aiden, this is my mother, Maria."

He extended his hand. "It's nice to meet you."

Maria waved away his offer, then wrapped both arms around him. The silver-haired woman was much stronger than he expected. Breaking away would not be easy.

Rosa giggled at his discomfort. "I should've warned you. She's a hugger."

"Too skinny," Maria said, finally letting him go. "Come. You no eat enough."

"Oh no! I'm fine. I—"

She disappeared into the house before he could finish.

Despite his hunger, McCrae was hesitant to follow. Sure, he'd spent three years eating slop. Before that, most meals had been grabbed on the go between jobs. And it's not like his mother had been one to prepare a nutritious dinner for her son each night. He would love a chance to sit down for a home-cooked meal.

But this felt eerily familiar.

The last time he'd been welcomed so openly was when the Council invited him to break bread and discuss his interest in joining the Commission. He'd been too trusting then. He wouldn't make that mistake again. Not with these people. Not with anyone.

But he couldn't be rude either.

By the time he shouldered through the crowded living room to join Maria in the kitchen, she'd already piled a paper plate high with tamales, rice, and beans. She steered him into a chair at the kitchen table, then stood over his shoulder like she planned to watch him eat.

The first bite hit like a sledgehammer. Heat ripped across his tongue, tearing through his sinuses like wildfire.

"Good?" Maria asked, her eyes twinkling.

After a single cough, McCrae reached for a pitcher of tea. "Yes, ma'am."

His reaction earned shy giggles from every corner of the room.

He ate with his head down as more neighbors arrived in drips and drabs. Rosa introduced McCrae to the new faces, though he had a hard time keeping everyone straight.

There was Jorge, a roofer with hands like leather.

His wife, Anna, still in scrubs from her shift at the hospital.

Their daughter, Sophia, an adorable nine-year-old with enough energy to power the block.

"How's Miguel?" Rosa asked. "Any update?"

Miguel Rivera. The lone survivor of the highway spill.

McCrae pretended to focus on his food while tracking every word.

"The doctors can't believe he's held on this long," Anna said.

"I pray he wakes while there's still time to save the others."

"Who needs saving?" Sophia asked. "I bet me and my friends can help."

"I'm sure you could."

"Well, not Sarah. She got the new iPhone for her birthday. She's had an attitude ever since."

This earned some subdued laughter.

"How's school going?" Rosa asked, directing the conversation to a child-friendly subject.

"Fine..."

McCrae smiled. The little girl had been speaking a thousand miles a minute only to shut down the moment she was asked to share details about school.

Some things really are universal.

"They keep telling her to speak English," Jorge said.

Anna drew a deep breath. "It's an easy thing to do, papi."

"On the playground? At lunch with her friends? She should speak however she wants."

Rosa caught Sophia staring uncomfortably at her plate. "Any cute boys?"

"No!"

These laughs weren't subdued.

The small house continued filling with warmth. Children ran in and out, allowing the screen door to slam despite adults yelling for them to stop. Teens shared viral videos on phones with cracked screens. Men argued about soccer as if they were alone in a barbershop.

An elderly man with sun-damaged skin approached McCrae with a Mexican beer in each hand. He stepped softly, using silent gestures to greet friends along the way. Once across the room, he offered a bottle to McCrae. "For helping today," he said, his accent heavy.

When McCrae took the beer, the stranger bowed his head. Then he was gone.

McCrae eventually found refuge in a cramped laundry room just off the kitchen.

A folding table was wedged into the corner beside a water heater on its last legs. A mess of political flyers was scattered across the square table. He found one with a long list of instructions written in Spanish.

Rosa appeared in the doorway. "That's how to respond if ICE knocks on your door."

His focus shifted to a stack of textbooks pushed aside like an afterthought. "Yours?"

Rosa reached past him, scooping the books into her arms and shoving them under the table. For the first time since meeting her, McCrae saw her confidence slip.

"I keep saying I need to sell these before they're out of date."

"Are you taking classes now?"

She shook her head, went a few rounds with her shame. "It was a waste of time, anyway. How many lawyers start out on a card table in the laundry room?"

He shrugged. "Looks like a decent origin story to me."

She was about to respond when the low rumble of multiple engines drifted into the house from outside. Rosa rushed into the living room. McCrae followed her, watching through the window as unmarked vans tore into the neighborhood.

Tires screamed against asphalt.

Then the van doors flew open, and armed men poured out.

"¡La migra!" someone screamed.

"¡Escóndanse!" another voice cried. "¡Rápido!"

The agents wore tactical gear over plain clothes. Black masks concealed their identities. While their vests had generic identification like POLICE or ICE, the men wore no badges and ignored all known procedures. Real cops announced themselves, showed warrants.

These assholes just tackled the nearest barrio resident.

The house erupted in chaos.

Jorge swept Sophia into his arms. Teenagers scattered toward the back exit, bare feet slapping against the worn linoleum. The elderly seemed torn between flight and the fear of abandoning family. The quiet man who'd thanked McCrae with a beer pressed himself flat against the wall as if he could melt into the wallpaper.

Maria stood frozen in the kitchen doorway, her weathered hands gripping the frame to stay upright. Her lips moved in silent prayer.

Rosa was the only one moving toward the front door.

"No!" McCrae shouted. "Wait!"

She was already gone.

Rosa lifted her phone, the camera already rolling. "Identify yourself! Show me your warrant!"

Boots ground one of those carefully sewn flag combinations into the dirt.

Still watching from the house, McCrae spotted a woman with a fistful of papers stumbling after agents dragging her teenage son toward an idling van.

"Wait! Please! He's American! I have papers!"

Rosa stepped directly into their path. "You don't even know who you're arresting!"

When the agents tried to brush past, she grabbed one by the arm.

"She has his birth certificate! If you just wait—"

A backhand caught Rosa flush across the jaw.

That's when McCrae put down his beer and stepped toward the door.

# TEN

Moments ago, parents were yelling for kids to stop slamming the screen door.

McCrae nearly took the door off its hinges.

The barrio was under siege.

ICE agents dragged zip-tied captives toward idling vans, boots pounding pavement, rifles sweeping porches and windows.

Doors hung open. Curtains twitched, then snapped shut.

Children screamed, raw cries that cut through the crack of shouted orders.

Women stumbled after husbands and sons, pleading for mercy in broken English and rapid-fire Spanish.

"Please—he's a citizen!"

"¡Mi hijo, por favor!"

An agent shoved one mother back with a forearm to the chest. She went down hard, palms slapping concrete.

A skinny teen in cargo shorts was being hauled off by two agents, his arms cinched behind him. A toddler chased after him, shouting his name.

"Why are you taking me?" he asked in a panic. "I don't understand. Talk to me, please."

Rosa pushed to her feet, ignoring the blood that trickled from a split lip. She was about to reengage when she spotted McCrae marching with purpose toward the nearest agents.

One agent saw him coming. "Stop!"

When McCrae didn't slow, he pulled a baton.

McCrae ducked, then drove a shoulder into the agent's chest. Followed that with a knee to his descending face. Cartilage crunched with a wet snap, and the agent dropped, his baton clattering across the asphalt.

A second agent's hand flew for his weapon. McCrae stepped in, using a palm strike to cave his throat before pivoting to whip him face-first into the van's side panel.

Steel boomed. The agent slid down in a boneless heap.

McCrae grabbed the fallen baton and backed into the mouth of a narrow alley between two homes, brick and shadow at his back as he waited for the next wave.

The alley was cluttered with everyday debris. Laundry lines sagged with clothes and faded sheets. Trash cans overflowed onto the pavement. A children's bicycle was abandoned, one wheel missing, the handlebars twisted at an unnatural angle.

The remaining agents moved as one, quickly fanning out to surround him. Six in all, exhibiting the same tactical know-how McCrae had noticed in the Home Depot footage. He couldn't assume these men were untrained like Castillo's crew back at Stateville.

An agent charged toward him. McCrae pivoted away and brought the baton down on his wrist. Bone snapped. The agent's scream cut through the chaos as an elbow to the temple took him down for good.

Two more tried to flank him, only to discover there was no room.

McCrae drove his baton into one's knee. The joint bent sideways with a sound like ripping canvas. Another scream. The next man stumbled over his partner, arms windmilling for balance. McCrae bounced his face off the brick and mortar of the nearest wall.

Another agent, younger, reached for his sidearm.

"No!" someone shouted. "No guns!"

McCrae was on him as the gun cleared leather. His right hand caught the agent's wrist and twisted sharply. The weapon barked once, a round sparking off the pavement. McCrae buried a knee in his groin, then wrenched the pistol free, snapping the agent's trigger finger.

The kid crumpled. He'd learned a valuable lesson, but he'd also distracted McCrae.

A blur knifed in at the edge of his vision. He snapped

his arm up, catching a baton with his forearm just before it smashed into his skull.

Pain lanced up McCrae's arm. He answered by burying his baton into the agent's gut.

The blow forced a high-pitched wheeze through the man's mask. Then McCrae seized his vest, spun him hard, and hurled him so he crashed into his recovering friends, their bodies tangling in the narrow space.

McCrae pressed his advantage amid the confusion. Blows slipped through his guard—ribs, shoulder, hip—but he absorbed them and responded with worse: a low kick to an exposed knee, a baton strike to the kidney, a sharp elbow to someone's throat.

"Pull back!" someone finally shouted.

No one looked ready to turn their backs on McCrae.

The same voice, harder now, called from the street: "That's an order! Fall back now!"

This time they obeyed.

McCrae watched them go. His forearm throbbed. His knuckles were already swelling. But beyond that, he'd escaped largely unscathed. Even better, he'd bought some time for the barrio residents to free their friends and family. He may have enjoyed the element of surprise, but a win was a win. And tonight, these black-bag assholes were going home empty-handed.

Several agents were helping the most seriously injured when McCrae noticed a keycard dangling from one man's shirt. He quickly snagged it, pinning the agent with a hard stare that dared him to object. The man staggered after the others without a word.

Once the vans peeled away, residents slowly emerged from hiding, peering around doorframes and through parted curtains.

Most ran to help the injured, dropping to their knees beside those still dazed or bleeding on the pavement. Others just stared at McCrae, their expressions a mix of gratitude and something closer to fear. He knew the look. Most people spent their lives ducking confrontation; they never knew how to act around someone who'd chosen violence.

Rosa appeared at his side. They stood in silence for a long moment. Then: "More YouTube?"

He grinned. "You okay?"

"Better than them." She gestured to the card in his hand. "What's that?"

McCrae studied the badge. Something was off about the hologram. It caught the light wrong. Too much shimmer, no depth. He ran his finger along the edge, found it was uneven as if cut by hand. Then there was the ICE logo itself. It was off-center. Not by much. Two millimeters, maybe. Most would miss it.

Just not a man who'd spent most of his adult life relying on fake IDs.

"It's blown," McCrae said.

"Huh?"

"The badge. It's fake. Good work, but definitely counterfeit. With a good printer and the right supplies, someone could make this in their garage."

"But why?"

McCrae had already connected the fake badge to their visit with Heller. Rosa, still trembling with adrenaline, needed a moment longer to piece it together.

"¡Carajo! That's why no one showed up in the database."

"Whoever took your friends out of the Home Depot parking lot, whoever dumped those bodies in the waste, it wasn't ICE."

"Who would do something so sick?"

The Commission. Judge Lambert was right to suspect their involvement. They were the only ones brazen enough to try something this bold.

And yet McCrae only shrugged, playing dumb. Rosa and her people already lived in a constant state of fear. He couldn't bring himself to tell her the ugly truth.

If anything, she and her people weren't scared enough.

# ELEVEN

McCrae's shoulder still hummed from the spot where a baton had glanced off bone, but it was the raw ache in his hands that bothered him. He sat with his knuckles submerged in a motel ice bucket. Each time he closed his eyes, he hoped to see anything but a replay of the blow that had put Rosa on her back.

It didn't work.

Why hadn't he stepped out of the house just a little sooner?

Once the throbbing settled to a dull ache, he pulled his hand from the ice, dried it on a thin towel, then opened the burner's encryption app and dialed out.

Two rings, then Judge Lambert's face filled the screen. She sat with her hands folded on an office desk. Mahogany bookshelves stood behind her, law volumes arranged with precision. An overhead light flattened the shadows under her eyes but couldn't hide them.

"Mr. McCrae," she said.

"Your Honor."

"I was beginning to worry you'd taken off on me."

"I saw no sense in risking a call if I had nothing to share."

"Does that mean you have something now?"

"I think I might."

He gave her the essentials—Kellner's debt, the forced midnight runs, Rosa's claim that the men found in the slag had been grabbed in a supposed ICE raid.

"Supposed raid. Why do you say it like that?"

"Immigration has no record of the men in their database."

Lambert shook her head and leaned forward. "That doesn't mean much. Those federal systems are a hot mess. It could be—"

"We sat down with an official in their office to confirm it."

"We?"

"Ms. Delgado did most of the talking."

Her eyebrow twitched. "Is that all?"

"No. ICE stormed the barrio earlier tonight. One of their men was carrying this." He produced the badge for the judge. "It's a fake."

"You're certain?"

He nodded.

"And he just happened to drop this crucial piece of evidence?"

"I may have... procured it."

Lambert's gaze drifted off-screen while wrestling with her frustration. "So someone's masquerading as ICE to kidnap migrants, only no one bats an eye because these fake raids look no different from the real ones."

"That's about right," McCrae said.

"But why? To what end?"

"If they were nabbing young women, the answer would be obvious. But they seemed to ignore them completely."

"How many people have been taken?"

"It's impossible to say. ICE has a presence in the area. They have taken people into custody. But there's no way to know who was apprehended legally and who wasn't."

"Well, how many people did they get tonight?"

McCrae chose his words carefully. "I suspect it was fewer than planned."

She leaned into the camera, her expression stern. "You aren't there to play vigilante."

"Would you rather I just let these frauds nab innocent people off the street?"

"The badge is the only proof you have that they weren't with ICE."

"And?!"

"Remind me again how you got the ID."

McCrae clenched his teeth. She'd caught him. He'd

stepped in long before he knew the whole thing was a production and the agents storming the barrio were fake.

"You're there to find a link to the Commission. That's all. Helping those people is admirable. I understand how easy it is to let your emotions get the best of you, but—"

"That's not what happened," he said sharply.

She steadied herself with a deep breath. "It wasn't an insult. Just a reminder that you're only one man. You can't ride in on a stallion to save everyone. If we're going to get results that last, we have to play the long game. That means you have to keep a low profile. You can't march into a federal building where every inch of the floor is covered by security cameras."

It was a point he had to concede. "Understood."

"Do you know your next move?"

"The badge has an embedded RFID chip. If it's active, it will be registered to someone."

"Send me the serial number once you have it. I'll see what I can do."

He pulled back from the screen, his shoulders stiffening. "Thanks, but I've got it."

A sad smile touched Lambert's lips. "Aiden, you may feel alone, but you're not. Not in this. I can be a resource if you let me."

He let the silence stretch. Then: "Are we done?"

"We are," she said softly. "Enjoy your evening—"

McCrae killed the call, and the screen went black.

He sat there a long time with the dead phone in his

hand, listening to the motel breathe around him—the rattle of ancient pipes, an argument leaking through wafer-thin walls.

He still wasn't sure he could trust the judge. Even if he proved she was on the level, he worried it would never be enough. As his fingers traced the cratered skin of his chest, he wondered if he could ever allow himself to trust her, if he could ever trust anyone again.

Feeling alone wasn't his problem.

His problem was that it was only in empty rooms like this that McCrae ever felt safe.

## TWELVE

After eighteen months, Dean Holbrook was growing wary of his partners.

He stood at the window of his temporary office, thumb grinding an anxious groove into the sill as he stared out over the waterfront wasteland he'd promised to transform.

The glass needed cleaning. Worksite dust coated everything for miles, even up here. But he saw enough. Cranes jutted from skeletal towers. Dump trucks crawled between containment zones. In the distance, the cleanup site glowed under sodium lights, its perimeter wrapped in privacy screening that concealed the real work from prying eyes.

From the beginning, his father had told him he was in over his head. Even now, he could hear him sneering through a thick haze of cigarette smoke. "You're an idiot to keep throwing money at these big-shot consultants. Those boys in Chicago can spot a sucker like you coming a mile away."

The old man didn't understand his son had ambitions beyond the portfolio of shoddy rentals he stood to inherit. He hadn't killed himself in B-school to spend his life shaking down Section 8 tenants for rent like his father.

He wanted more, and the Commission had shown up just in time to help him get it.

It had been a chance encounter that had led to his first sit-down with the Council. They'd told him the Commission was ready to go legitimate, to move from backroom deals to boardroom negotiations. More importantly, they wanted the Riveton waterfront to be their first flagship venture. Holbrook would continue to be the project's face. Meanwhile, the Commission would be the invisible hand working behind the scenes to get things done.

And they'd done exactly that.

People who wouldn't take Holbrook's calls were suddenly leaving messages for him. He was awarded status as a preferred bidder on the project. Out of nowhere, state reps were promoting his vision on the local news. Competitors dropped out with no explanation. It was like someone had flipped a switch. It all happened so fast that Holbrook never thought to ask how it was getting done. And why would he? His new partners had given him something he'd chased his entire life...

The chance to prove his father wrong.

Even if a few arms got twisted along the way, Holbrook knew his competitors were doing the same. So when the Council came to him with an opportunity to bring in non-union labor that would save millions, he didn't blink. He just assumed they had a plan to pay the crews under the table like everyone else.

It was several months before he realized no one was getting paid at all.

The service elevator groaned, its doors opening to reveal Holbrook's security team.

Well—what remained of them after their latest efforts to round up workers.

Knox limped, his left knee swollen to the size of a grapefruit. Beck's nose was crooked beneath swollen eyes. A gash over Shaw's eye wouldn't stay closed.

Holbrook didn't understand. These weren't mall security guards. They were contractors from a top-notch security firm. Guys with special forces experience. They were supposed to be the best, but all of them were moving with the slow shame that comes after an ass-kicking.

It was easy to imagine his father getting a good laugh at that.

Garrison stepped out last. The Commission called him an operator, someone sent to oversee their investment in the waterfront. He rarely raised his voice above regular conversation, never wasted a gesture. But he carried himself like a man who might snap at any moment, violence coiled tight beneath the tailored suit.

"What happened?" Holbrook asked.

Garrison gestured for Knox to answer.

Knox cleared his throat. "We hit the neighborhood for new recruits. Things started smoothly. We had half a dozen lined up to bring back when some asshole stepped in to play hero."

"You're saying one man did this?"

The men shifted uncomfortably.

Holbrook forced a sarcastic laugh. "Maybe we should look into hiring him."

"Maybe," Shaw said with a sneer.

"How many were you able to bring back?"

All around him, eyes dropped to the floor.

"None?! You people are getting paid like doctors. You're telling me if I brought in some ass-wiping CNAs, I would have gotten the exact same result?"

"Perhaps you'd like to show us how it's done," Shaw said, his tone shifting from suggestion to dare.

Holbrook felt the room tilt. He'd pushed too far. But he couldn't allow Shaw to have the last word. Not in front of the others. For a second, he considered firing Shaw on the spot.

But he never got the chance.

Garrison was already moving to handle it.

The operator moved like a blade through water, his hand clamping around Shaw's neck.

The others slid aside as Garrison steered Shaw across the room. He tossed Shaw into the corner, watching him slide down the wall before popping the lid on a bin of industrial waste. It had been set aside to serve as a visual aid during an upcoming inspection of the project.

Garrison had different ideas.

He shoved Shaw face-first into the bin. Gray dust billowed up, the stench of burnt metal and battery acid filling the air. Shaw tried to break free, his legs kicking violently.

Holbrook stepped forward, his mouth opening to intervene. Then he caught the flat look in Garrison's eye, and any intervention died in his throat.

Garrison pushed Shaw's face deeper into the sludge.

One second.

Two.

Three.

When he finally let go, Shaw came up gasping, black foam bubbling from his lips.

The rank smell made bile rise in Holbrook's throat.

Garrison looked to the rest of his team, his eyes moving from face to face, daring anyone to object. They met his expectant gaze with silence.

He found a shop towel and brushed loose dust from his sleeve. When he noticed Shaw had spewed black sludge onto his shoe, he wiped it clean.

"Go home," he said. "Heal up. Expect some heavy work ahead."

His men nodded before limping toward the elevator. Shaw managed to stand, one hand braced against the wall. His breathing sounded like wet gravel in a blender. No one moved to help him until Garrison gave approval with a slow, quiet nod.

"We'll have to push the men we have a little harder while we work to get this ironed out."

"They're barely upright as it is," Holbrook said.

"In the meantime, we have a mess of our own to clean up."

Holbrook's stomach sank. He'd been worrying that the subject of Miguel Rivera would come up again. "I want no part of that."

"You're only there to run interference with the family."

"It feels like an unnecessary risk. I'm told there's little chance he comes out of his coma."

Garrison laid a heavy hand on Holbrook's shoulder. "You're with the Commission now. We don't leave things to chance."

He followed the others out. Holbrook watched the elevator doors slide shut, his father's old warning drifting on the stench curling out of the open container.

*Those boys in Chicago can spot a sucker like you coming a mile away.*

As he turned toward the window, toward the nefarious work unfolding below, Holbrook quietly wondered if the Council's perch above the city had given them an advantage over everyone else. Maybe his father was right.

Maybe the Commission had seen him coming before anyone else could.

## THIRTEEN

Only a few businesses on Bell Street were left breathing. Each wore the same armor—steel grates, reinforced glass, cameras watching everything. That's what it took to survive on this side of town. The rest waved flags of surrender, FOR LEASE signs yellowing with age.

Rosa pulled to the curb outside Dolan's Pawn and Loan. The split lip from last night's confrontation had scabbed over, but she kept touching it with her tongue like she couldn't believe it was real.

"You sure about this?" she asked.

McCrae studied the shop squatting beside a shuttered nail salon. A sign in the window read WE BUY GOLD - BEST PRICES. Below that, in smaller print: LICENSED FFL DEALER.

"He'll have what we need," McCrae said.

"Okay, but if he doesn't—"

"No one's getting hurt today." He opened the passenger door but stopped short of climbing out. "Well, no one's going to get hurt this morning."

They pushed through the shop's reinforced door, setting off an electronic chime.

Dated electronics crowded the shelves. Guitars clung to pillars. Power tools filled locked cages along one wall. Jewelry cases held a wide variety of gold and silver—mostly wedding rings.

Behind the counter, a man looked up from an ancient desktop computer. Late sixties, sun-damaged skin, a patchy beard in need of a trim. His eyes tracked them with the patient calculation of someone who'd learned to read trouble before it announced itself.

"Can I help you?"

McCrae approached the counter, noting the framed Army patches on the wall behind him. "This your place?"

"That's right. Hank Dolan, owner/operator."

McCrae produced the counterfeit ICE badge. "Do you have anything that will read the information on this chip?"

Dolan stared at the badge without touching it. "Tell me you're not one of them."

"No, sir."

"Good." He took the badge, turning it over in his weathered hands. "I voted for border security, not this Gestapo bullshit."

Rosa looked ready to blow until McCrae used a gentle

touch on her arm to keep her from jumping down the old guy's throat.

"Didn't know I'd have to watch Paul Vasquez get dragged out of his own garage. He's been fixing cars in my neighborhood for twenty years. Only charges people what they can afford. Helps down at the church. They wouldn't even let him say goodbye to his kids."

Rosa reeled in her annoyance. "Does his family know where they took him?" she asked softly.

"Detention center in Florida. His brother hired some high-priced immigration attorney. Not sure that will do much good, but they're taking hope where they can get it."

"He may be one of the lucky ones."

The lines across Dolan's brow deepened. "How you figure that?"

"I have friends who have vanished without a trace. No detention centers, no court dates. Just—*poof*—gone."

Dolan met her eye with genuine remorse. "I'm sorry."

"But," McCrae said, "this badge might help us understand why."

"Then we'll see what we can do."

The old man disappeared into the back for a moment, eventually returning with a device that looked a lot like a cashier's barcode reader.

"Not sure this will work, but we'll give it a go."

He waited for a green light to illuminate before scanning the badge. Nothing happened. He adjusted several settings, blew dust off the ID's embedded chip, then tried again.

All he got was more of the same.

"If the badge is fake, won't the chip be a knockoff too?" Rosa asked.

"Probably," McCrae said. "But if they're using these cards to scan in and out of a security checkpoint somewhere, they may have made an amateur mistake."

After a few more adjustments, Dolan swiped the chip again.

This time, the scanner chimed.

"Well," he said excitedly. "Hello there."

"What do you got?" McCrae asked.

"Just a UID number. 445-7892-XX3. Not sure we're gonna get anything else."

McCrae already had his phone out. "That's all I need."

He typed out a message for the Judge with the UID number.

"Now what?" Rosa asked.

"She's waiting for it, so it shouldn't take long."

Rosa shot him a confused look. "Who?"

He shook his head as if the answer didn't matter.

Ten minutes later, McCrae and Rosa were sitting on worn stools, fingers wrapped around Styrofoam cups gone lukewarm. The shop had settled into a heavy quiet—no customers, no traffic, just the slow tick of a dozen wall clocks marking the awkward silence.

Working behind the counter, Dolan kept glancing their way like he still wasn't sure what to make of them. McCrae checked his phone half a dozen times before there was a message to read.

Lambert's response: *Meridian Solutions, LLC. Researching now.*

"Okay," McCrae said. "We've got something."

Another buzz. *Corporate registration shows 1847 Slate Way, Riveton.*

Rosa turned pale after McCrae finished reading the messages aloud.

"That's HPG," she said.

"Who?"

"Holbrook Property Group. They own half the barrio. Every broken heater, every leaky roof, every rent increase that's forced good families into the street."

"I thought Holbrook was the guy with all the signs promising to save Riveton."

Dolan laughed, short and bitter. "Junior won a contract to turn the old steel mill into one of those mixed-use developments. Half the developers in this state were vying for a piece of that one on account of the government funding."

"How much?"

"$660 million."

The developers weren't the only ones who would want in on that action. The Commission loved gaining leverage over large-scale construction projects. Each offered a hundred ways to skim without leaving fingerprints. The fact that this one was backed by the Feds only made it better. No one throws money at a sinking ship like Washington.

"Does Holbrook have any experience working on something so big?" McCrae asked.

"Hell no," Dolan said. "He promised to get the cleanup done in three years. Even if he had the backing to invest in all the safety protocols—which he don't—he'd need an army working 'round the clock to get that done. I don't know one person who's gotten hired on."

"You're kidding?"

The old man shook his head. "They've got these big screens raised to block everyone's view. When they drop, I bet we find they haven't accomplished a Goddamned thing."

The pieces were coming together now. The illegal transport of toxic waste. The emaciated bodies found in the sludge. The fake ICE raids targeting working-age men.

The Commission had built an empire exploiting desperate people.

Now they were snatching them off the street.

McCrae's voice came out flat. "He's using them for labor."

"What are you talking about?" Dolan asked.

"That's why the bodies in the spill showed signs of extended exposure. They'd been worked to death."

Not all of them, though. There'd been one survivor. Miguel Rivera. That poor boy in the hospital was a loose end waiting for the Commission to tie up.

"O-okay," Rosa said, panic rising in her voice. "We've gotta take this to the police, right?"

"We can't."

"When they see what we have, they'll go out to the site and see what's happening."

"You're talking about the same people who didn't lift a finger to investigate what happened to your friends in the spill. No, most of the local cops were bought and paid for long ago."

"Well—we have to do something!"

"You're right," McCrae said. "We have to get to the hospital to protect your friend."

## FOURTEEN

Rosa led McCrae off the elevator when it arrived on the fourth floor.

The ICU always hit different than the rest of the hospital. Harder lights. Sharper sounds. Ventilators forcing air into reluctant lungs. Nurses speaking in hushed tones that suggested death was lurking just around the corner.

Rosa found the Riveras sitting quietly in a cramped waiting room. Rosary beads clicked through Mrs. Rivera's fingers, steady and precise. Her husband stared at the wall, work-worn hands folded in his lap.

But it was their guest who made Rosa come apart at the seams.

Dean Holbrook had beaten them to the hospital. Only they hadn't caught him with a pillow pressed to Miguel's face. Instead, he was seated beside Mrs. Rivera, one hand resting gently on her arm as if he were an old family friend.

"I have friends with resources for situations like this," he was saying, his voice carrying the warmth of a funeral director. "Medical bills, legal assistance. Whatever your family needs, don't hesitate to ask. I can put you in contact with the right people."

Rosa seethed as she closed the distance between them.

Holbrook looked up, his expression shifting seamlessly from compassion to mild surprise. "Ms. Delgado. It's good to see you. I wish it were under different circumstances, but—"

"You mean circumstances you didn't create?"

Her raised voice drew concerned looks from the nurse's station down the hall.

Frustration flickered behind Holbrook's thousand-watt smile. He leaned close to Mrs. Rivera, whispering something before giving her hand a reassuring pat. Then he rose to his feet and guided McCrae and Rosa away from the grieving couple.

"Let's not cause a scene. I'm sure you're here to console the Riveras the same as me."

Rosa pulled the counterfeit badge from her pocket. "Have you told them about this?"

He summoned a puzzled look to his face. "Are you going to tell me what I'm looking at?"

"ICE agents were carrying these during a raid on the

barrio last night. Only we both know that isn't the whole story, don't we?"

The developer fell back on his heels. It was only a slight shift in weight, but McCrae knew to watch for the universal tell. An involuntary retreat was often the body's confession.

Holbrook's face hardened. "You've become a leader in your community, Ms. Delgado. You've earned that. But this kind of reckless behavior can be dangerous."

"Is that a threat?"

"Just an observation. Leaders who stir up panic sometimes end up as headlines. I'd hate to see that happen to you."

McCrae had heard enough to know he was right. And he couldn't let a comment like that slide without offering a warning of his own. He was ready to push his way into the conversation when a figure started toward them from down the hall.

A familiar face.

Ray Garrison.

McCrae knew Garrison as a guy who'd made his nut boosting trucks out of Milwaukee. Apparently, his star was on the rise if the Commission had trusted him to serve as their operator in Riveton.

Would he recognize McCrae?

More importantly—did this mean they were too late?

A bedside alarm punctured the silence.

A nurse frowned, then rose to waddle down the corridor toward the alarm's source.

Then the tone sharpened.

BEEEEEEEEEP.

The flatline wail that meant a heart had stopped.

"Code blue, ICU room 412! ¡Código azul, UCI habitación cuatro-uno-dos!"

The hallway erupted in controlled chaos.

A crash cart thundered around the corner as hospital staff materialized from nowhere, moving with practiced urgency toward room 412.

A primal cry escaped Mrs. Rivera's lips, a sound so raw it seemed to shake the walls. Her husband lurched to his feet, but his legs looked ready to come apart at the joints.

A nurse caught them both in the doorway, forcing the couple to watch from a distance.

Holbrook lowered his head, the picture of polished sympathy. "Tragic."

Garrison joined him. "No," he said, voice flat. "Clean."

That single word confirmed what McCrae already feared. This wasn't a patient losing a fight; it was a witness being erased.

The crash team fought to bring Rivera back. Compressions, intubation, medications pushed through IV lines, but McCrae knew it was all a waste of time.

There was no remedy for an air bubble in the heart.

Holbrook led Garrison away, both walking with the ease of men who believed they were untouchable, confident that even if suspicions were raised, nothing would stick.

As they rounded the corner, Garrison's focus found McCrae.

His stride never broke; his expression stayed smooth.

But his eyes narrowed just enough for McCrae to know that his cover was blown.

## FIFTEEN

McCrae checked the time. Twenty minutes. Still no response from Lambert.

He placed another call, his third.

Straight to voicemail. Again.

He'd found privacy in a tiny chapel wedged between the ER and the cafeteria like some kind of afterthought. Light filtered through a stained glass window behind the pulpit, painting the dimly lit space in fractured pools of color.

The door creaked when Rosa entered to join him. Her adrenaline had burned away, leaving her with the hollow-eyed exhaustion of fresh grief. But there was something else. Her movements were more careful, more deliberate. She wouldn't quite meet his eyes.

It was the way a person approaches a stray dog they worry might bite.

When she reached him, she didn't sit.

Even before she spoke, McCrae knew something had changed.

"He's gone." Her voice was steady, even if her hands weren't.

"I'm sorry," McCrae said softly.

She gripped the pew beside him, her knuckles losing color.

Through the wall, someone was crying.

"You'll have to get somewhere safe," McCrae said. "It wasn't smart to show our hand like that. We should have—"

"How did you know they would come for him?"

McCrae sensed her gears were turning. "A hunch."

Rosa finally turned to look at him. "Was it?"

His shoulders squared as if instinctively bracing for an attack. "Your friend was the only person who could confirm what happened to those men. That made him a liability."

"And what about the guy with him? You knew him, right?"

"Why would you think that?"

"The way you looked at him. The way he looked at you. What did you mean by crooked cops?" She watched his reaction as if she knew he wouldn't answer. "You told Heller you'd known your fair share of crooked cops. That's a really weird thing to say."

He couldn't believe his need to get the last word in with that prick was coming back to haunt him now.

"I've been thinking about these last two days," Rosa continued, her words growing in strength. "It's not just the way you fought off those agents. It's how you handled Heller. The way you immediately knew the badge was a fake."

"Any bartender can spot a fake ID."

"Who were you texting in the pawn shop?"

McCrae shifted his attention to the stained glass window where an armored knight stood with his sword lifted toward the heavens.

"I brought you into my home, Aiden. Introduced you to my mother. I *shared* things."

"Both things meant more to me than you will ever know." Saying this left McCrae feeling more exposed than he cared to admit.

"Then tell me you're not here to babysit me," Rosa said.

His throat tightened. "What?"

"Tell me you aren't here to make sure I stay one step behind."

"I promise I'm here to bring down these assholes the same as you."

"But you didn't know Mike Kellner, did you?"

Rosa continued searching his face for the truth, her focus so intense he nearly broke.

"Who are you?" she asked. "Who are you really?"

His phone saved him with the buzz of an incoming call.

Rosa started down the narrow aisle, moving with purpose as she disappeared through the door. He wanted to go after her, to come clean about everything. But when his phone buzzed again, McCrae answered the call.

Judge Lambert's face filled the screen. "Where are you? Is that—is that a church?"

"Hospital chapel."

"Jesus. I told you—"

"I'm alone. Besides, we have bigger problems. I think I may have been made."

This pulled her to the edge of her seat. "How?"

"Ray Garrison. An operator for the Commission."

"Did he say anything?"

"He wouldn't under the circumstances."

"What circumstances?"

"Rivera's dead. Garrison killed him."

Confusion creased her brow.

"The chip you ran was registered to a shell company connected to a local developer named Dean Holbrook. Holbrook was awarded a government contract to clean up the contamination at an old factory site to make room for a waterfront development. I think the Commission is helping him stage fake ICE raids so they can round up free labor."

"And if Rivera had come out of his coma—"

"He could have confirmed all of this to be true."

She needed a moment to process everything she'd learned. "A few years back, the DEA found immigrants being held against their will at a weed farm in Oregon. Same thing. They were being used as slave labor, too."

"So who do we contact to see a raid like that in Riveton?"

"That isn't the plan," she reminded him. "We don't have enough, anyway."

"How the fuck can you say that?"

Lambert flinched.

"We have witnesses who claim the victims were taken in an immigration raid, but the government has no record that the raid took place. We have a manufactured ICE badge that we've linked to the Holbrook family. I'm sure tests would confirm the waste in the spill matches the shit being removed from the waterfront. What else do you need?"

"My friend needs something with teeth, something to interrupt everyone's doom scroll. Otherwise, we risk the story being replaced by whatever rage-bait conspiracy the algorithm chooses to push next."

"You're talking about pictures," McCrae said.

"Video is better."

"Video."

"If you're really made, we need you back in your cell before the Commission gets the chance to see that you're gone. That cuts your time in Riveton by a day. This is your last night to get us what we need: footage so haunting people can't look away."

"And the people posing for this family movie?"

"They'll have to hold on a little longer."

"So I'm supposed to document suffering, not end it."

The Judge sighed. "Aiden, you've done everything I asked. Please—"

"Your girl will get her footage."

The chapel felt colder after ending the call.

McCrae studied the stained glass until the full scene came into focus: the knight was positioned between a quiet village and a coiled serpent, sword lifted to strike.

This arrangement with the Judge still made no sense. If she only wanted pictures, why not hire a private investigator? Why risk her career to let a convicted killer loose on the streets?

As he replayed their meeting, McCrae realized he'd already stumbled onto his answer.

Lambert had called him the only man with the skills to bring the Commission down. What was that, if not a polite way of saying she expected him to deliver a kind of justice no court could? Even the people who'd built this quiet sanctuary seemed to understand that the fight between good and evil often demanded more than thoughts and prayers.

The serpent in its window wasn't being captured, after all.

It was being slain.

## SIXTEEN

The foundry had once been Riveton's heart—a roaring furnace that pumped prosperity through the city's veins and shipped steel to the rest of the world.

Now it looked like a malignant growth waiting to spread.

Buildings of crumbling brick sagged along the riverbank. Rust-eaten arches and half-collapsed catwalks stitched one ruin to the next. Smokestacks that had once belched fire into the sky now leaned at awkward angles.

Holbrook had thrown up a chain-link fence topped with razor wire. The privacy screening Dolan described was erected to block any view of the property's ground level. Still—McCrae had seen enough on his first pass.

Two guards at the main gate, each with a holstered sidearm. Another pair patrolled the perimeter. They didn't move like your standard rent-a-cops killing time until their selection exam. They maintained spacing. Checked their six.

The shitty high-and-tights sealed it.

Mercs.

If Holbrook had done the hiring, they were likely from a top-flight outfit like Aegis. If he'd been advised by the Commission, they were most likely Onyx Shield. Onyx men came with a stiffer price, but most had left their morals buried in some desert halfway around the world. They would turn a blind eye to anything if the check cleared.

Even slave labor.

McCrae hugged the shore, hidden from view as he made his way toward a drainage tunnel that cut beneath the fence line—three feet of corrugated steel, rusted and forgotten.

The tight space left him with one option. He'd have to crawl along on his belly.

The smell hit first—chemical runoff mixed with decay, a stench that clung to the back of his throat. The tunnel pressed in from all sides, gray water sloshing around him.

Something sharp snagged his jacket, tearing the fabric.

He pushed forward, dragging his knees and elbows across rough metal. He felt like he'd been shimmying along forever when the darkness finally gave way to a dim light ahead.

McCrae hoisted himself up through a grate into a

building's sub-basement. The dank room was crammed with dead machinery from another age. Seized gear assemblies, drive belts gone to rot, control panels with needles frozen at zero.

Light leaked through an open doorway at the top of a rusted staircase. Sounds carried down from above. Orders barked in English. Answers in Spanish, thin and broken. The scrape of shovels on concrete. Wet, ruined coughs.

It was the soundtrack of weak men forced into hard work.

McCrae started up the staircase, testing each step before trusting it with his full weight. He crouched near the top, melting into the shadows before easing forward to steal a look at the main floor.

What he saw made his chest feel like poured concrete.

His suspicions had not prepared him for this.

Hispanic men in tattered clothes and paper masks were working under halogen floodlights. They shoveled contaminated soil into drums. Sorted through debris with hands protected by threadbare gloves. Dumped solvent into massive storage containers that released visible fumes into the air.

They moved as if their bodies could give out at any moment.

Open sores wept through their clothes. One man's mask was dark with blood.

Six guards supervised from behind the protection of hazmat suits, each armed with a cattle prod.

A frail worker stumbled, dropping his shovel. The guards gave him two seconds to recover before lighting him up. He convulsed, screaming through his paper mask before finally reaching for his shovel with trembling hands.

This was the footage Lambert was after.

A nearby guard shifted position, his gaze sweeping past McCrae's hiding spot.

McCrae pressed himself flat against the wall, barely breathing. When no one came, he opened his phone's camera and lifted the device to record. Only the angle was all wrong. He needed elevation, distance. He couldn't capture the scope of the operation from this vantage point.

McCrae waited for the nearest guard to look away before darting across the floor, low and fast. He slid into hiding behind a forklift just as the guard's attention swung back around.

From the vehicle's driver's seat, he could finally get it all.

He was nearly done recording when movement near the north wall stole his attention—two guards escorting workers shuffling toward an open shipping container.

When the workers stepped inside, a guard chained the doors.

McCrae circled around, using more of the heavy equipment as cover. As he drew closer, he nearly gagged on the stench wafting out of the container: human waste, sweat, disease. The smell of bodies crammed together and dying slow.

He peered through the gap between the container doors. A dozen men were trapped in the darkness. Soiled blankets and makeshift pillows littered the floor. A bucket in the corner served as the group's only latrine. All the men showed signs of chemical exposure—rashes, lesions, skin peeling away in sheets.

McCrae had seen suffering. He had caused plenty himself. This was different.

The Commission had graduated from breaking legs to committing genocide.

He snapped several pictures, backing away once his phone was heavy with evidence. Lambert had wanted something visual—something visceral enough to cut through the social media noise.

If this didn't, nothing would.

He was mapping a route back toward the basement stairs when he spotted a crumpled form, another discarded body left to rot like the ones pulled from the highway spill. He shook his head, ready to move on.

Then the man's chest rose.

Just one breath, but unmistakable.

McCrae froze.

The man's eyes fluttered open and found him.

"Ayúdame." The raspy plea came through cracked lips.

McCrae's path to freedom was wide open. He had his

proof. Enough to save hundreds, maybe thousands, from a similar fate. The phone in his pocket would be the first shot fired in his private war to bring the Commission down, to slay the serpent. But if Lambert really wanted something with teeth, there was one thing with even more bite than the footage he'd recorded.

A survivor with a story to tell.

McCrae dropped to one knee and eased the man upright. The worker weighed almost nothing, skin drawn tight across bone. "Can you walk?"

The man nodded.

Then his head sagged as if he were too weak to hold it up.

McCrae draped the worker's arm over his shoulder. The man's legs moved in an awkward shuffle. Each step drew a wheeze from ruined lungs.

The heat felt worse now, the fumes thicker. McCrae's throat burned. He'd only been here twenty minutes and already felt sick.

How long had these poor souls been breathing this poison?

They'd covered half the distance to the basement stairs when McCrae spotted a guard posted near the landing. Stopping for the survivor had cost him an easy escape.

Now he had to find an alternative.

The main gate was out; too many Onyx men. The north exit meant scaling a razor-topped fence. Even if his new friend could make the climb, they'd be torn to shreds. That left—

His passenger coughed.

"Quiet," McCrae hissed.

The man doubled over, his body betraying him with a coughing fit that echoed across the floor. McCrae looked out to find three guards already converging on them.

He scanned for a weapon: a pipe, a crowbar, a fucking shovel.

Nothing.

He'd have to do this the old-fashioned way.

He led the sick man into hiding, then doubled back to stalk the guards. They'd split up, no doubt confident they were pursuing a sick worker they could easily handle on their own.

The first guard passed within arm's reach. McCrae slipped from the dark, his forearm locking around the man's throat. The hazmat suit made for a difficult takedown—too much material, too little leverage—but steady pressure on the carotid finally got it done.

The guard sagged into unconsciousness. McCrae lowered him soundlessly to the floor.

Another guard came around the forklift, cattle prod humming with blue fire.

McCrae waited. Patience often separated professionals from corpses.

When the guard turned a blind corner, McCrae

exploded from the shadows, driving a shoulder into the man's gut.

But the big bastard barely budged. He grappled McCrae, dragging him across the floor until they smashed into a steel drum. The impact rang through the foundry like an alarm bell.

The guard slashed the air with his prod. Missed by inches.

McCrae grabbed his mask, then slammed his face into the drum's rusted rim.

Plastic cracked. Blood spurted from behind the shattered respirator.

McCrae finished him with a shot to the kidney.

He was just turning to find the last of the three when lightning tore through his spine.

Every muscle seized. His vision flared white. Pain roared through him, his nerves misfiring so he was no longer in control when his body hit the ground.

A boot crushed his hand, grinding bone against concrete. When McCrae finally yanked himself free, it was just in time to see the crackle of blue fire come streaking toward him again.

## SEVENTEEN

Holbrook had to get his hands around this thing before it all slipped away.

He watched Knox and Beck haul the intruder into the cramped office and drive him to his knees. Their hoods were shoved back. The man's wrists were already raw where the zip ties had chewed into his skin.

Holbrook was still deciding how to play this when the intruder lifted his head—and Holbrook realized he recognized the face. "Hold on. You're the quiet guy from the hospital. The one with the waitress."

The stranger said nothing, instead letting his eyes sweep across the empty office of some mill supervisor long since dead. Black mold caked the few remaining ceiling tiles. A forgotten desk sat in the corner, drawers rusted shut, the surface crusted with petrified rat shit.

"How did you get past the gate?"

Silence.

Holbrook turned to the guards. "Is this the same guy from last night?"

"That's him," Beck said. "Wasn't so lucky this time around."

"You should have left well enough alone. I was ready to write that off as a man who got caught up in the moment. Now that you've come poking around, I have to assume it was more. Does Delgado know you're here, or was this—"

"Aiden McCrae." Garrison slipped through the door behind them, a thin smile caught somewhere between amusement and concern. He made a slow circle around the prisoner, careful to study him from every angle. "So that really was you, huh?"

"You know this guy?" Holbrook asked.

"McCrae here was the Council's golden boy for a long time. Until he grew a conscience. As I understand it, that became... inconvenient." He turned to the guards. "We'll move him into the city first thing tomorrow. For now, take him to the old fabrication building. Whatever you do—"

"Wait," Holbrook said. "Y-you aren't going to question him?" He hated the waver in his voice.

"Eventually. But the Council will want some answers of their own."

"Then they can have him when we're done."

Garrison's gaze hardened to steel. "Is that what you'd like me to tell them, Dean?"

The room seemed to shrink around Holbrook. He felt the guards waiting to see if he'd fold. His mind raced in search of a response, something sharp enough to remind Garrison of his place.

The operator waited him out. When Holbrook offered nothing more to fill the silence, Garrison gave a thin smile and stepped out the door.

Heat crawled up Holbrook's spine. Knox and Beck shifted in the silence, plastic suits crinkling, boots grinding through decades of grit. Beck suddenly found the corroded desk very interesting.

The intruder's voice finally broke the silence. "You do realize there's zero chance you get this project over the finish line, right?"

Holbrook spun on him, grateful he finally had a new target for his rage.

"They'll treat the waterfront like it's their personal piggy bank," McCrae said. "Stolen equipment, no-show jobs, fake invoices for companies that only exist on paper."

Beneath the stranger's calm voice, Holbrook heard his father's judgment bleeding through: *You're out of your league. This is a game for serious people, not you.*

"You don't know what you're talking about." Holbrook tried to lower his voice, but even he could hear it—he sounded like a man trying to convince himself.

The Council had promised the Commission was going legit, that their investment in him would be the foundation of a new era for their organization. Had it all been a lie? Had the plan always been to carve up his project and sell it for scraps?

Even worse, had it already started?

Just last week, the solar panels for their temporary generators had vanished. And the consulting firm Garrison had insisted he hire? Holbrook had been cutting them monthly checks since February, but he'd yet to meet with anyone from the company.

What exactly was he getting for that money?

"They're going to bleed you dry."

The hint of pity in McCrae's voice only stoked Holbrook's fury. "Shut up."

"And when people ask why Riveton's savior failed so spectacularly, when the media destroys the Holbrook name, that's when they'll make you disappear."

"Enough."

"It's what they do. They've got radar that lets them lock in on a mark like you."

This landed so close to home that Holbrook briefly thought he smelled the same cigarette smoke that always accompanied his father's low, belittling rasp. "I said enough!"

His hand moved before his brain caught up. The slap cracked across McCrae's face, snapping his head sideways. Pain flared through Holbrook's palm. He stood there, breathing hard, staring at his own hand as if it belonged to someone else.

Something cold settled in his chest. He turned to the

guards. "Forget what Garrison said. Take him past the county line. Lose the body somewhere it won't be found."

The guards hesitated.

"Do I have to remind you who signs your checks?"

"No, sir," Beck said.

They hauled McCrae upright, but before they could shove him through the door, Holbrook stepped in to block their path. Giving the order wasn't enough. They needed to see this wasn't a desperate move to save face.

Holbrook had to prove he was in complete control.

"You're wrong," he said. "We haven't even broken ground, and the Commission has already introduced me to some overseas trade partners. In fact, we're meeting one tonight who's eager to tap into my... labor pipeline."

McCrae smirked. "Is that what we're calling it?"

"Of course, they don't need workers so much as... inventory. Young inventory. Female." Holbrook let that sink in, then added lightly, "Your friend from the hospital, Ms. Delgado. She's so passionate about her community work. You think that will translate?"

McCrae's restraint evaporated like water on hot steel. He surged forward, but Knox and Beck wrenched him back before he could take a full step.

Holbrook recoiled, his heart jackhammering. "Get him out of here."

It took both men, muscles straining, to drag McCrae through the doorway.

## EIGHTEEN

The guards marched McCrae through the foundry's toxic heart.

Workers kept their heads down as the trio passed. Around here, it was likely that stopping to witness another man's fate would only invite trouble. Knox kept the cattle prod visible, while Beck maintained a vice-like grip on McCrae's arm.

Once outside, the cool night air was a relief after the chemical-heavy heat in the building.

In the lot, several Onyx Shield mercenaries appeared to be performing a final weapons check. Others were loading into the unmarked vehicles.

Were they really planning to storm the barrio again?

Beck waited for Knox to yank open the rear doors of an idle cargo van before tossing McCrae inside. With his wrists bound, McCrae's shoulder absorbed most of the impact, sending fresh spasms through muscles still twitching from the taser.

He rolled onto his side to watch his captors climb into the front. There was no barrier between the empty cargo bay and the cab.

Gravel crunched beneath the van's tires as they rolled through the gate, then smooth asphalt announced their arrival on city streets.

"These two need to establish a chain of command," Knox said from behind the wheel.

Beck answered from the passenger seat, "We should take this to Garrison."

"Do what you want. I'm listening to the man whose name is on the sign out front."

McCrae rose into a seated position, bracing his back against the wall as he tested the bite of his nylon restraints. He slowly fed his bound hands past his hips, one inch at a time, careful to keep his movements so slight they were masked by the van's sway.

"You talk like losing this gig is the worst thing that can happen."

"And?"

"You don't find this to be a little fucked up? I don't care if they are illegal."

"At least I don't have to worry about any of these boys strapping a bomb to their chest."

The restraints caught on McCrae's belt. He twisted his wrists, wincing when the nylon sliced deeper into his skin and drew blood. It was only when he got his hands under his thighs and past his knees that the tension loosened enough to give him some relief.

When they slowed for a turn, McCrae swept his boots through the loop of his arms in one fluid motion. His wrists remained cinched tight, but with his hands in front of him, he wasn't as helpless as he had been just minutes ago.

*Young inventory. Female.*

He saw Rosa's face. The easy trust when she'd walked him into Maria's kitchen, the hard suspicion in the hospital chapel. She'd been right to be wary. If only her instincts had been a little sharper from the start, maybe she wouldn't be a target now.

The van slowed at a red light.

McCrae didn't wait for a complete stop.

He shot forward between the seats.

"Oh shit!"

Beck's surprise was punctuated by the crash of Knox's skull being driven into the steering wheel. The horn blared—a short, angry blast. Blood splattered the dash. A second impact split Knox's eyebrow open to the bone.

The van rolled through the red light, cutting off a Kia that swerved to avoid it.

Beck twisted in his seat, his bulk working against him in the confined space. McCrae snaked his bound arms over the big man's shoulder and cinched them across his throat.

Beck's meaty hands tore at McCrae's forearms. He had raw power, but McCrae had leverage.

Right up to the moment when the nylon restraints finally snapped.

The sudden release sent McCrae tumbling backward onto the van's floor. Beck gasped, one hand clawing at his throat while the other searched blindly for a weapon.

Knox came alive. He jerked the wheel to avoid the concrete pylons guarding a bus stop. Then he reached across his body for the pistol under his left arm.

McCrae found his feet and pushed forward again.

His freed hands found Knox's wrist just as the Glock cleared its holster.

The first shot punched through the van's roof. The report was deafening in the metal box, the muzzle flash filling the cramped interior with white light.

A second round blew through the windshield, spider-webbing the glass.

McCrae wrenched the pistol sideways. Knox's trigger finger snapped with a wet crack, drawing a hoarse scream from his lungs.

The van jumped a curb. A parking meter disappeared under the front bumper with a metal scream. They sideswiped several cars parked outside a dive bar called SECOND SHIFT.

McCrae was ripping the weapon away from Knox when a massive hand from the passenger seat found his throat. Its fingers were like iron bands crushing his windpipe. He couldn't breathe. Blood flow to his brain had all but stopped. Dark spots clouded his vision.

He'd been on the other side of this more than he cared to admit.

He knew he had only a matter of seconds before blacking out.

McCrae raised the Glock, but Beck caught its barrel and drove it toward McCrae's face. With teeth bared, McCrae fought to hold it off with the last of his strength.

But it wasn't enough.

Beck was too strong. McCrae was growing too weak.

His only chance was to stop resisting.

The shift in balance sent Beck lurching forward, overextended. His forearm came within range. McCrae dropped his full weight on Beck's arm, trapping it against the hard edge of the armrest. The joint held for a second—then failed.

A deep, splintering crack tore through the cabin.

Beck's howl shook the van. His grip loosened just enough for McCrae to slip free.

His lungs screamed for oxygen, but he couldn't waste his chance. He turned the Glock on Beck. It spoke once, painting the dashboard in red mist.

Finally gasping for air, McCrae collapsed onto the van's ridged floor.

His ears rang. The zip ties had turned his wrists to hamburger. His throat felt crushed, each breath whistling through damaged cartilage.

But his pain could wait.

Rosa couldn't.

McCrae dragged both bodies into the van's cargo hold. By the time he was finished, two men had stepped from the bar to assess the damage done to their vehicles.

"Look at this motherfucker," one said.

The other saw McCrae climbing behind the wheel. "Hell no! Your drunk ass ain't fixin' to run."

He moved in to block the vehicle's path while the other started toward the driver's side door.

Both men dove aside when McCrae stomped on the accelerator.

One of them hammered a fist into the side panel as the van fishtailed away. The other stumbled into the street like he planned to chase him down on foot.

McCrae kept his eyes on the road, letting the drunks shrink in the rearview. He didn't have time for them. Holbrook's men could roll into the barrio any minute.

It might have helped to ask for directions, though. He may have been in a race to save his friends, but as the speedometer climbed past fifty, the truth finally hit him.

McCrae wasn't even sure he was headed the right way.

# NINETEEN

The engine screamed as McCrae pushed it to its limits.

He'd taken three turns that felt right, but the unfamiliar streets kept folding back on themselves like a maze designed to trap outsiders.

He was wasting time he couldn't afford to lose.

McCrae finally saw a corner that felt familiar. He yanked the wheel, tires squealing. This was right. He was sure of it. He was going to make it to the barrio in time, to the people who'd opened their home to him, to the old woman who'd fed him, to Rosa.

But all he found was more of the same.

More shuttered storefronts, more slum duplexes, more shadows and darkness.

He punched the steering wheel. "God damn it!"

Then—static.

A burst of white noise came from somewhere inside the van.

McCrae searched the cab in confusion, his gaze eventually settling on the sound's source: the center console.

He steadied the wheel with one hand so he could pop the console open. He dug through the debris: fast food wrappers, a broken vape cartridge, tangled charging cables.

Then his fingers landed on a two-way radio buried beneath the trash.

Voices crackled through the radio's speaker as McCrae lifted it from the console.

"—Alpha team in position."

"Copy that, Alpha team. Blake, what's your status?"

The chatter from Holbrook's men was crystal clear. That could mean only one thing.

McCrae was close.

"Good to go," someone said through the radio.

"Then we're moving on my count. One, two, three."

McCrae listened to the shuffle of boots across concrete; the jostle of tactical equipment.

Then came the crash of a battering ram over the radio.

A door splintering. An explosion of shattered glass. A woman's scream in his ear.

"On the floor! Everybody on the fucking floor!"

McCrae's knuckles turned white on the wheel as he listened to Spanish voices rising in terror.

Dogs barking. Children crying.

"We've got a runner!"

"Back door! Back door! North through the alley!"

Ragged breathing. The sick thud of bodies colliding.

A sharp cry—young, female, desperate.

"Got her!"

"No! She's just a child! Please!"

McCrae finally saw some familiar landmarks through the window.

"Another down!" someone shouted through the radio. "That's three secure."

"Make that four."

"This one makes five!"

He heard zip ties ratcheting tight. Bodies being thrown into the empty cargo space of a van.

"That's it. We're rolling."

The last broadcast from the radio was the slamming of vehicle doors, the hum of tires over asphalt. Then it went quiet for good.

McCrae swung into the barrio to find he was too late. Most of Holbrook's convoy was gone. Only one van lingered at the curb.

There was no room on the narrow street to swing around and fall in behind it.

So McCrae buried the gas pedal instead.

He was still accelerating when he T-boned the escaping van.

Metal screamed. Glass exploded. The impact slammed McCrae into the steering column, knocking the air from his lungs.

Steam poured from McCrae's hood as both vans skidded to a stop, locked together in a crumpled knot of steel.

McCrae fumbled for the Glock, shoved his door open, then staggered into the street. The other driver sagged behind the wheel, barely conscious, face slack with shock as he pawed at a blown airbag. McCrae used the pistol's weight to knock him out for good.

With the driver subdued, McCrae rounded to the rear, tore the latch free, and flung the doors wide. A teenage girl sat slumped against the wall, wrists bound, hair matted with blood.

But she was alone.

McCrae turned to assess the state of the neighborhood.

Children drifted in the street—some crying for parents, others silent as they wandered aimlessly. A wailing toddler waddled with a diaper drooping between his knees. Mumbling prayers in Spanish, a woman pressed a dishtowel to her husband's bleeding scalp.

Most simply stood where they were, frozen.

The survivors tracked McCrae as he moved through the block. He saw grief, despair—but there was something else too, something unexpected. Some were glaring at him.

He pushed past it, his attention shifting to Rosa's house. María stood in the doorway, one hand braced against the frame as if she believed the house might collapse without her.

McCrae hurried up the walk, took every step at once.

"Easy," he whispered. "I've got you."

She didn't seem to hear him.

He took her tiny hand and guided her onto the porch. She moved like someone wading through the remnants of a bad dream. McCrae righted a fallen lawn chair and helped her to sit. When her gaze finally found him, the tightness in her shoulders broke.

"Where's Rosa?"

Tears cut fresh streaks down her cheeks. She tried to speak but only shook her head. For McCrae, that was answer enough.

Jorge stepped through the screen door, shirt torn at the shoulder.

McCrae rose quickly. "Sophia?"

"She's fine," Jorge said, his voice raw. "Anna too. We've got a safe room. But Rosa..." He faltered. "She had time to hide, but the Hernández boys... their father works late."

"So she went to help them."

There was nothing more to say. Both knew there'd be no stopping her. If anything, catching a backhand in the last raid had made her even more likely to intervene.

"They've never gone after our women," Jorge said. "Why now? What changed?"

"It was him!" A neighbor stumbled to the fence between their yards, her housedress hanging loose. "My Ella is thirteen. Thirteen. They take her now because you fight back!"

Jorge tried to calm her. "Eso no es cierto."

She dropped to her knees, sobbing.

An old man marched up the driveway, fury carving deep lines into his face. "¡Tú! ¡Esto es tu culpa!" The Spanish was like fire from an assault rifle.

"¡Abuelo, no!"

A young man hooked an arm around him before he could reach McCrae, but he couldn't prevent the accusations from flying. "¡Él trajo esto sobre nosotros!"

McCrae didn't need a translation. Blame sounded the same in every language.

And who's to say he was wrong?

People in McCrae's orbit had a funny way of getting hurt. Maybe he was more toxic than the poisons being scraped out of the foundry. Maybe the universe had decided his sins carried interest that could only be paid in the suffering of anyone foolish enough to stand close.

If so, that was one debt he would not pay.

He knew what became of women trafficked overseas. The lucky ones died quick. The rest lived out a nightmare worse than anything those men found in the highway spill had faced.

He started into the street, back toward the crashed vans, ready to carve a path through as many men as it took to ensure that wasn't the end of Rosa's story.

Lucky for him, there was already one within arm's reach.

## TWENTY

McCrae dragged the driver into an abandoned house by his collar. The Onyx Shield merc was only now awake enough to realize his hands were zip-tied behind his back.

"What the—motherfucker, do you know who I am?!"

"I do," McCrae muttered.

"Good! Then let me go, and maybe I won't kill you where you stand."

McCrae kicked the door shut, then shoved him to the floor in the nearest corner. The empty living room stank of mildew and old smoke. A sheet of plywood was nailed over the front window. Someone had punched holes in the drywall to strip out copper pipes and wire.

"You and I need to have a conversation first."

The driver sized up McCrae, his eyes snagging on the Glock for a half-second before he dragged his gaze up to meet his captor's eye. "You think you can intimidate me? I've been trained to endure shit you can't imagine."

McCrae tipped his head toward the glassless window. "I don't know," he said. "Those boys outside sound awfully eager to prove you wrong."

A chorus of angry voices was building in the front yard. Clearly, word was spreading that one of the men who'd stormed the barrio hadn't made it out with the rest. That fake ICE vest might as well have been a bullseye strapped across his chest.

And yet, the driver remained steady. "I'll take my chances with them before I turn on the Commission."

"Right now, you should worry about me."

The mercenary smirked. "We'll see. It's not as easy as you think. Hurting a man who can't defend himself. It requires you to go to a dark place most men can't."

McCrae slid the Glock into his waistband and dug a phone from his pocket. Not the burner. This was a phone he'd lifted off the merc before dragging him in from the wreck.

"You must be a second-stringer," he said.

"Second-stringer?"

"It's hard to believe that the top contractors are dumb enough to take their personal cell phones with them on missions into the desert."

"Good luck getting it open. I don't use that face lock shit."

"I've got everything I need in this picture," McCrae explained.

The lock screen's background was a family portrait—the driver, his wife, a young daughter smiling into the sun like the world had yet to show her its teeth.

Seeing McCrae so focused on the picture finally put a crack in the merc's bravado.

"Cute kid."

"Hey! You even think to threaten my family—"

McCrae feigned surprise. "Stop. No one's getting hurt. Any punishment I dole out is going to fit the crime. I'd only hurt someone you care about if you hurt someone I cared about. You didn't do that." His tone went ice-cold. "You sentenced her to a life of sexual slavery."

The driver surged to his feet. McCrae easily kicked him back to the floor.

"She's twelve years old, you sick fuck!"

"You have any idea how valuable that makes her?"

The merc lunged again, wild and desperate. McCrae let him run straight into a right jab.

"Don't worry," he said. "It will only feel like forever."

The driver spat blood onto the stained carpet. "Fuck you!"

"You'll spend a few years searching, praying you find her. But you'll eventually give up. Fathers say they won't, but they always do. You'll choke down guilt while trying for another kid to save your marriage. And when you've finally clawed your way back to a life that feels half-ass normal, when you finally think you've put this behind you—that's when you'll wake to find your prayers have been answered, and your little girl's been dropped on your doorstep, all used up with a needle in her arm."

This landed harder than any punch could. People liked to say the worst part of a child's disappearance was not knowing what had happened.

McCrae knew better.

"You think you've been to dark places? You ain't seen nothing yet."

Outside, a young man shouted something in Spanish, his voice sharp with rage. Others answered. The mob seemed to be swelling.

"You want me to leave you with them while I go check in on your family?" McCrae asked.

"It's bullshit," the driver muttered, more to himself than to McCrae. "You don't have it in you."

Someone pounded on the front door like they meant to take it off the frame.

"Several of your buddies have died tonight. You think your wife will bring your daughter to the funerals, or is she more likely to leave her at home with a sitter—or alone?"

Anger erupted from within the mercenary. "God damn it!"

"Tell me where the girls were taken and what kind of resistance I can expect."

The driver held on for a moment before finally giving in.

"They aren't being held," the driver said, more fight draining out of him with every new word. "We were told to take them directly to the exchange."

"Where?"

"An old shipyard. Two miles downriver from the foundry. The buyer's supposed to come in off the water. He plans to move the girls straight to a ship that's already en route. Pier C."

McCrae studied him, searching for any sign he might be lying.

When he saw none, he started for the door.

"Wait," the driver said. "How 'bout cutting me loose?"

"You'll have to take that up with your new friends," McCrae said.

"Son of a bitch!"

The driver lurched to his feet, stumbling toward the back of the house in search of an exit.

When McCrae stepped onto the sagging porch, the knot of young men in the yard surged forward as if they meant to run him down. Yesterday they'd been kids trying to look tough; now the pack mentality made them dangerous.

"¡Ya basta! ¡Atrás!" Posted on the top step, Jorge was the only thing keeping them penned in the yard.

"Thank you," McCrae whispered.

"You get what you needed?"

"We'll know soon enough."

"Good. I'm not sure how much longer I can keep these boys back."

A couple of kids had pistols jammed into their waistbands; the rest were filled with enough blind rage to ensure their hands were the only weapons they'd need.

"Just hold them off long enough for him to get a head start."

"What?" Jorge snapped. "Why?"

"Because your people have lost enough as it is."

Confusion pinched Jorge's brow, but McCrae didn't have time to explain.

He took one last look at the house, the threats he'd made inside looping through his head. He felt no shame in doing what it took to get answers. What rattled him was how easily he'd gone there. There'd been a time when a gun felt wrong in his hand, an awkward weight.

Now it seemed like violence was the only answer he knew.

Moving through the yard, he quietly hoped the driver would make it out safely. Not for his sake. That bastard had sold his soul long ago and deserved whatever came to him.

His hope was for the soul of this neighborhood.

If the barrio got hold of the driver—if those angry boys were allowed to put hands on him—this block would never be the same. That's why most people stayed away from places so dark. You can't walk into them without leaving a piece of yourself behind.

## TWENTY-ONE

McCrae eased the van into the alley behind Dolan's Pawn and Loan, then killed the engine.

He slipped out of the vehicle and moved along the cinderblock wall, stopping at the back door. The steel looked thick enough to stop small-caliber rounds. Two deadbolts gleamed in the amber glow of a streetlight. He drew a breath and crouched to study the locks.

Nothing so elaborate that the picks Lambert provided couldn't get the job done.

He eased the slim case from under his jacket. It was always hard to trust new tools—all shine and sharp edges, no history. So he kept it simple, choosing a stiff tension wrench and a plain hook pick. Nothing fancy. Nothing that made promises it couldn't keep.

He set the wrench and listened.

Two blocks away, a wailing cat sent a trash can clattering. Beyond that, tires squealed.

McCrae ignored both. He kept his breathing slow, closing his eyes to heighten his other senses. The wrench turned fractions of a degree; the pick whispered across pins, each scrape a note in a tune only he could hear.

Then—*click*.

Top lock, done. Like he hadn't lost a step.

But the second put up a fight.

Sweat sheeted his brow. This so-called work release had turned into a straight endurance trial. Adrenaline was the only thing keeping him on his feet, but even that was running low.

He adjusted the pressure and eased the rake. The night static of a shady neighborhood continued to crowd him—a bottle skittering across asphalt, an angry dog barking in the distance.

The lower bolt finally surrendered with a tired snick.

He lowered his tools. He was about to open the door when—

"Hope you aren't too attached to that hand."

McCrae turned, freezing when he saw the black eye of a shotgun staring back at him.

His chest flared hot and tight, scar tissue knotting as if the wound were fresh. For half a second, he thought he was beaten again. Then Hank Dolan emerged from the shadows, and the fear loosened its grip, leaving only that phantom pain behind.

"Turn slow, son. Don't test an old man with nothing to lose."

McCrae put his hands in the air with his palms open. "I know better than that."

Recognition softened Dolan's glare into a look of confusion. "Well—son of a bitch. You're the boy who came by to scan that badge."

"Aiden."

"Shame. I liked you."

"Good. Because I need your help."

"Too late for that."

"Not if you give me a chance to explain." McCrae eased forward.

Dolan steadied the weapon. "Right there will do."

"Fine," McCrae said, fighting to keep his voice even. "But listen. There's a reason you don't know anyone who's been hired on at the waterfront. Holbrook has been staging fake ICE raids—kidnapping migrants and forcing them to work cleanup at the foundry."

Dolan snorted. "That boy doesn't have the sack."

"His partners do."

"And who's that?"

"The Commission."

Dolan had been around long enough that the name meant something. His shoulders sagged, eyes drifting as if he were looking into the past. When he spoke again, his tone had lost its edge. "They're using the president's hard-line immigration policy as cover."

"Exactly."

"Okay," the old-timer said, blinking himself back to the moment. "But that still don't explain why you're picking my lock like a man who's done it a thousand times before."

"It looks that way because I have. But that's not why I'm here. Holbrook's taken my friend, and I'm gonna need some serious firepower if I'm going to get her back."

"Her?"

"The Commission's not satisfied with free labor. They've cut a deal to trade young women for building supplies. A few of these girls are barely in their teens."

Dolan shook his head, disbelief hardening into disgust. "And here I thought his old man was a piece of work."

He finally lowered the shotgun.

McCrae felt a wave of relief. He was beginning to worry Dolan would force his hand.

The back room was a rectangle of poor lighting and good steel. A pegboard of neatly hung tools covered one wall. A scarred counter ran beneath it, marked by decades of work.

Dolan slid the deadbolts, then leaned his weapon in the corner. "You strike me as a man who knows what he's looking for in a firearm."

"My only need tonight is something that comes with ammunition," McCrae said.

"You're going to need a lot more than that."

McCrae sensed where the old man was going. "This is something I've got to do alone."

"I'm not sure you're in a position to turn down help. Besides, I may not look like much, but I've still got a few tricks up my sleeve."

Dolan walked to a wall hung with fishing rods and vintage signs advertising motor oils and brake pads. He slid two rods aside and pressed his thumb against a notch in the trim. There was a soft pop. Then the panel swung out to reveal a narrow set of plywood stairs descending into darkness. Fluorescents hummed to life when Dolan hit a switch. The staircase groaned under their combined weight as they started down.

"Damn," McCrae said when he came off the last step. "You weren't kidding."

Dolan seemed to stand taller down here, shoulders coming back in a subtle shift that indicated he was glad to know he might be taken off the shelf again.

He'd built a nice little doomsday cache with bottled water, canned goods, and vacuum-sealed bags of dehydrated meat. Enough supplies to last him for months. A locked cabinet brimmed with blister packs and orange prescription bottles. A plywood shelf sagged under tattered paperbacks—Ludlum, Clancy, Child—books men read when they needed to remember there were still men willing to walk through hell in the name of what's right.

And then, the reason they'd come: the weapons.

Two gun safes stood open, AR carbines leaning

shoulder to shoulder like soldiers in formation. Pistols lined the top shelf—Glocks, SIGs, and a few wheel guns that would never jam.

On a nearby workbench, Dolan kept his tools arranged like surgical instruments: cleaning rods, bore brushes, and a reloading press fitted with dies for multiple calibers. A mason jar overflowed with spent brass, each casing scrubbed bright as a new penny.

Dolan gestured to the gun safe. "Pick your poison."

McCrae eventually landed on a compact AR-15-style carbine: short barrel, collapsible stock, thirty-round mag. Plenty of reach across a yard, no problem chewing its way down a hall.

"That will work," Dolan said. "Now for the star of the show."

He pulled a crate onto the bench, popped the latches, and opened the top to reveal blocks of C4 nestled in foam like eggs in a carton.

McCrae arched a single brow. "You know how to use that stuff?"

"Like riding a bike." Dolan dug out a long coil of det cord and two radio detonators. His hands moved with muscle memory, checking connections, testing circuits.

McCrae was eager to move, but he slowed to watch Dolan slide into a bulletproof vest. The old man's fingers fumbled slightly with the straps—arthritis or adrenaline.

Probably both.

"Thank you," McCrae said softly.

Dolan held his gaze, answering with a quiet nod before tightening the vest around his chest. "You say they're shipping these girls out tonight?"

"They're supposed to meet the buyer at a shipyard a few miles north of the foundry."

"I know it," Dolan said. "This girl—she the one that was with you today?"

McCrae answered with a nod.

"She's got some fire in her belly. She'll hold her own for a while."

The old man started up the narrow staircase.

McCrae lifted his carbine, checked the chamber, then let the bolt snap forward. He wanted to share Dolan's confidence, but he knew a woman like Rosa would provide a different pleasure for some men. They'd see her as a spirit to break.

They had to get on the road before the flame that made Rosa special went cold for good.

## TWENTY-TWO

Holbrook cracked the SUV's window. Night air crept in, thick with algae and diesel fumes. Through the windshield, the shipyard docks stretched out in hard angles. Cranes rose like gallows against the night sky. Containers were stacked six high. Black water slapped concrete with the steady tick of a metronome counting down to someone's demise.

He shuffled the papers in his lap: safety certifications, progress reports, worker contracts with signatures he would never match to faces. All of it ammunition to shoot down any concerns during next week's inspection of the waterfront.

All of it fake.

All of it provided by the Commission.

"We good?" Garrison asked from behind the wheel, his voice barely rising above the engine's idle.

"They'll work," Holbrook said.

Garrison tracked a forklift crawling across the pier. "You're learning."

Holbrook stared through the glass, his jaw tight. He'd graduated summa cum laude from Northwestern. Networked his way into Chicago's power circles. Transformed his father's collection of low-income rentals into a real estate portfolio approaching respectability.

Why did these people think they could keep talking down to him?

He circled back to what McCrae had told him.

*They're going to bleed you dry.*

The Commission might see him as a hog to fatten before slaughter, but it wasn't going to go down like that. He'd proven his father wrong. He'd do the same with the old men sitting around that ridiculous table high above the city in the Westlake Hotel.

He'd already ignored Garrison once when he'd sent those men to kill McCrae. But that was only the beginning. After they put this night behind them, he was going to remind everyone that the original pecking order had not changed.

Headlights swept the cabin as a cargo van turned to descend the ramp onto the pier. Garrison was already out when it rolled to a stop twenty yards away. Holbrook set the documents on the center console. Once he was sure no one was watching, he took a pistol from the glove box and tucked it into his waistband before climbing out of the car.

His palm left a damp print on the leather when pushing to his feet.

---

The stolen van was on its last legs and barely got them to the shipyard. By the time McCrae eased it to a stop, the temperature gauge was flirting with the red.

He and Dolan took the high ground—the tar-paper roof of an abandoned warehouse overlooking the north end of the yard. The building sat just outside the perimeter fence, providing them with an unobstructed view of Pier C, its docks, and the main access roads.

McCrae swept his binoculars across the shipping terminal. Fifty yards of open concrete separated a maze of stacked containers from a squat watchtower near the water's edge.

Holbrook waited at the base of the tower, bracketed by two vehicles—a black SUV and a windowless van. Garrison directed the Onyx Shield mercs into a loose perimeter. It was no surprise to see he was now running point. Even from a distance, McCrae could see Holbrook fidgeting, all nervous energy and restless hands, like a shy boy at his first dance.

It wouldn't be long before the Commission took complete control.

"Two men in the tower," Dolan said. He adjusted the scope on the bolt-action Remington he'd brought from his armory. "That's where they're keeping the women."

McCrae shifted his focus to the tower windows. He saw a flash of terrified faces in the glass, but a guard quickly ushered them away. There were no signs of Rosa among them.

"Six more on the deck," Dolan said. "That makes eight by my count."

McCrae mapped routes through the labyrinth of containers. Stacks of steel boxes carved half the yard into tight corridors—towering walls of rusted metal that would provide solid cover for most of his approach. But the last stretch was nothing but open concrete. Out there, he'd be target practice for the tower guards.

"I say we wait for the buyer," Dolan said. "That way they bring the girls to you."

"He's likely to have his own men," McCrae explained. "We're outnumbered as it is."

"Unless we can turn them against each other." Dolan shouldered his duffel of C4. "If I can get a charge set to blow the lights, that might be enough to pucker an asshole or two."

McCrae considered it. These exchanges were normally wound tight as piano wire. Even hardened pros would get a little twitchy if Dolan could rock the pier like he said. All it would take was one person to assume betrayal for the whole thing to go sideways.

He gestured to a ramp that connected the pier to an access road. "Meet me near the gate. Only don't blow the lights until you know you can get the van in position. Getting them away from the guards is pointless if we've got nowhere to go."

Dolan looked ready to respond when the throaty rumble of twin engines cut him short. A speedboat appeared through the fog, its sleek hull carving a wake toward the shipyard.

The old man shoved McCrae toward a ladder off the roof. "You better get moving, son."

The speedboat's whine grew steadily louder as McCrae descended through the shadows. When his boots hit the ground, he took the carbine rifle into his grip and slipped between the nearest containers. By the time he reached his final position, McCrae was just sixty yards from Holbrook and the rest of his heavily armed welcome committee, arriving just in time to hear the boat's engine die with a gurgle as the overseas buyer reached the pier.

## TWENTY-THREE

Holbrook held his breath while watching them step off the boat.

The buyer was smaller than expected—five-seven, maybe, with skinny wrists and narrow shoulders that didn't fill his blazer. But the two men flanking him were built like Russian tanks: thick necks, heavy hands. One had a crude spider tattoo crawling down his throat, its inked legs disappearing under the collar.

Garrison cast an unsettled look toward the stacked containers, then swept the dark shoreline for threats before stepping in beside Holbrook to meet the approaching men.

"Breathe," he said. "It will be over before you know it."

"I'm fine," Holbrook snapped.

His tone earned a concerned look from the operator. "Easy. Don't—"

Done listening, Holbrook stepped forward before he could finish, forcing his hand out to the buyer. "Dobry vecher," he said, the Russian syllables coming out stiff but serviceable.

The buyer stopped two feet short of the handshake. He kept both hands buried in his pockets. "Who are you?" he asked, his heavily accented words catching slightly.

"Well... I... should we really use names?"

The Russian scanned Holbrook as if assessing a piece of equipment that might fail inspection. When his eyes came up, he did not look impressed. "You are not Commission."

"I suppose not."

"Then why do you waste my time with your bullshit?"

"Because we're going to be working together. Relationships are everything in business."

The buyer turned to Garrison, eyebrows lifting in a silent question.

Garrison shook his head, acting as if the awkward exchange wasn't worth discussing. "Bring them out," he called.

Was that it? They were just going to ignore him?

The tower door banged open. An Onyx man appeared on the landing with a line of women packed in behind him. Wrist restraints, bare feet on metal. One woman sobbed openly; another was propped up by her friend. Only Rosa Delgado had any fight left in her.

"Let her go!" she said. "Can't you see she's just a child?"

The buyer drifted closer, eyes tracking the group as they clattered down the stairs. He studied them with the calm patience of a predator choosing which throat to bite.

When they hit concrete, one woman scanned the area in quick, panicked jerks. The others kept their gazes low, as if avoiding eye contact would make it all go away. Once again, Delgado was the only one with her chin up.

As they were herded across the pier, she locked onto Holbrook and never looked away. No pleading. No fear. Just a defiant stare that crawled under Holbrook's skin, cold and deliberate, until it felt less like resistance and more like a threat.

It was bad enough being nudged aside by the others like some errand boy. Now he was supposed to stand there quietly and let some truck-stop waitress eyeball him, too?

"Everything to your liking?" Garrison asked, his voice flat.

Fingers brushed a cheek here, lifted a chin there. When the Russian stopped near Rosa, she met his eyes as if she were memorizing his face for later. The buyer seemed to appreciate that she had some grit.

With a greasy smile, he looked back at Garrison and finally answered with a nod.

"The Council will be in touch," Garrison said.

Holbrook couldn't believe it. None of them would even be here if not for him, but it was becoming clear that the Commission meant to cut him out at every turn.

Unless he stepped in to retake control now.

The buyer muttered something to his brutes. The big men peeled away from him, moving with the bored efficiency of guys preparing to load freight. The women shied away, even more frightened of these two than the heavily armed mercenaries from Onyx Shield.

"Hold on," Holbrook blurted. "There are still some details we need to hammer out."

Every eye swung his way, the sudden attention settling on him like extra weight.

"What are these details?" the buyer asked, his accent thickening.

"Steel is steel. But now that we've seen the quality of the merchandise you're receiving, I think we need to renegotiate terms."

Garrison glared at him. "What the fuck are you doing?"

Holbrook barely heard him. He barely heard anything over his father's voice.

It was always his father's voice in moments like this.

For a long beat, no one spoke. Then the buyer huffed a low, disbelieving laugh. "This is the deal on which we agreed. I will not renegotiate on the dock of this dirty river in your dirty country like some filthy fishmonger."

"Then you can walk away," Holbrook said. "Something tells me I'll have a much easier time replacing you than you will replacing me."

The buyer's temper snapped. Russian poured out of him, hard consonants like broken glass. His men stiffened—shoulders squaring, hands drifting toward concealed weapons.

Garrison stepped forward, palms out like a man trying to keep the peace. "Easy. Let's everyone just take a beat. First off, Dean does not speak for the Commission."

"That's right," Holbrook said. "They reached out on my behalf. A deal doesn't happen without my approval." His hand moved to the small of his back, fingers closing around the pistol's grip. "And I'll blow up a shitty deal before I let you get the better of us."

He drew his weapon.

No one moved. The air seemed to thin.

It wasn't the gun that froze them—it was where he aimed it.

Even the waitress finally flinched when she saw herself staring down the barrel of his gun.

---

Still tucked in a corridor between stacked shipping containers, McCrae's grip tightened on the borrowed carbine rifle. "What the fuck?"

He was already beginning to worry he'd have to move before Dolan's signal.

Now Holbrook had a gun in Rosa's face.

"You really going to burn everything down over a pissing contest?" Garrison asked.

"They're the ones who'll walk away empty-handed," Holbrook said. "Not us."

"You kill our relationship with them, you're killing your relationship with the Commission."

Holbrook deflated briefly before throwing his shoulders back again. "So be it."

McCrae's odds had not improved. The tower guards were out of their nest, but that didn't help; they'd just folded in with the Russian heavies and the Onyx Shield mercs already strung along the perimeter.

He ran the rifle's stock out, welded it to his shoulder, and tried to settle his sights on Holbrook.

He couldn't find an angle. Not for a kill shot. And he needed a kill shot. Anything less, and Holbrook's reflex reaction might splatter Rosa's brains across the pier.

What was taking Dolan so long?

Maybe the old man wasn't as sharp as he thought. Maybe an Onyx guard had caught him creeping around a junction box and put him down before he could lay a single charge.

The plan was supposed to be simple: Dolan blows the lights, panic does the rest. In the dark, anxious men with guns assume betrayal and turn on each other.

But if that wasn't happening, McCrae needed another way to light the fuse.

Maybe there was a way to turn the Americans against each other instead.

He collapsed the carbine's stock and slid the rifle under his jacket. Up close, anyone with eyes would notice the bulk riding against his ribs. But from a distance, he might get a few seconds before someone called it out.

Seconds were all he needed to get that pistol out of Rosa's face.

It felt like a suicide mission, but there was no time to plan something better. So McCrae took a deep breath, let it out slowly to steady his hands, then stepped from the maze of shipping containers and walked onto the pier.

## TWENTY-FOUR

The spider-necked Russian saw him first.

His hand flashed under his jacket, the pistol coming up as he barked a warning and took aim. Onyx rifles followed, snapping toward McCrae in unison.

Garrison slashed a hand through the air. "Hold! Hold your fire!"

McCrae stopped with thirty yards of open concrete between him and Garrison. His pulse hammered, but he kept both hands loose at his sides, shoulders relaxed, acting like he was just a civilian who'd wandered onto the wrong pier.

When he saw McCrae, Holbrook's arm sagged as if the pistol had doubled in weight. By the time he caught himself, the muzzle was already off Rosa.

Rosa didn't waste the opening. Never bothering to see

who'd drawn their attention, she stepped in front of the others, putting herself between the men and the girls.

"I'll say this," Garrison shouted across the pier, "you certainly live up to the hype."

"Your boy made it easy on me."

Garrison's easy posture hardened. He turned toward Holbrook, slow and deliberate. "What the fuck is he talking about?"

Holbrook's polish was gone. His mouth worked soundlessly before he finally managed, "He's seen everything. It made no sense to leave him alive."

The buyer grumbled in Russian, his eyes darting back and forth between them.

Garrison didn't bother with a response.

He took two measured steps toward Holbrook. "Let's get one thing straight. You're here to be the public face of this thing. That's it. You don't make decisions. Not anymore. If you've got a problem with that, we can address your concerns anytime—"

A muffled blast kicked the pier beneath their feet. A shockwave rolled across the shipyard, rattling steel and blowing out warehouse windows. The overhead lights flickered off in a stuttering chain reaction down the docks until the shipyard was swallowed in darkness.

The buyer boiled over, harsh Russian shredding the silence like shrapnel. His heavies snapped their pistols toward the nearest Onyx guards.

The mercs reacted on instinct. Their rifles swung off McCrae and locked onto the Russians.

This time, it was Holbrook who tried to play peacemaker. "Wait! Everyone just—just calm down! It's not what you think!"

Rosa seized the moment, nudging the girls into motion, guiding them in a slow, shuffling tide toward the watchtower.

McCrae eased a hand toward the AR riding under his jacket.

"It's just a transformer," Holbrook insisted, desperation bleeding into his sales pitch. "These buildings are a hundred years old. The electrical—"

The next detonation ripped that story to pieces.

A white-hot blast punched out of the fuel depot, kicking open a doorway into hell. Fire ballooned into the sky, painting the yard in violent light. A crane shrieked as its steel failed, the boom folding in on itself and crashing down in a storm of sparks and twisted metal.

"Look out!" someone shouted.

The falling rig sent everyone scrambling for cover. Heat rolled across the pier in a scorching wave, the air thick with burning diesel and pulverized concrete.

Apparently, Dolan had decided to call an audible, too.

Whatever trust had existed between Holbrook's men and the Russians burned away in the firelight.

Gunfire erupted to fill the void.

McCrae pulled his weapon and spun toward two guards who'd circled to a position behind him. He dropped to one knee. His weapon spoke once. The shot caught the first guard center mass and lifted him off his feet.

He rode the recoil into his next target.

The second guard was about to adjust his aim when McCrae put him on the deck.

McCrae bounced to his feet and sprinted across the pier. Automatic fire shredded a dented dumpster. Sparks flew off a massive boat propeller as he blew past it.

Surrounded by the strobe of muzzle flashes, Garrison was hauling Holbrook toward the SUV. The developer had collapsed in on himself, forearms over his head as if that would stop rifle rounds. Garrison pulled a pistol and fired several shots blindly down the dock before climbing behind the wheel of the SUV and peeling away with Holbrook.

The kidnapped women huddled against the watchtower, five shadows pressed tight to the concrete. Rosa shielded the smallest, a sobbing girl who looked no older than a high school freshman—if that.

*My Ella is thirteen. Thirteen. They take her because you fight back.*

The neighbor's voice knifed through his head.

McCrae shoved the memory down and pushed toward the tower.

A merc clocked him, realizing too late they were being hit on two fronts. He swung his aim.

But McCrae was already there.

He drove the carbine's stock into the guard's temple. Bone gave with a dull crack, and the mercenary fell to his knees. McCrae kicked him onto his back, then flattened the man's face beneath his boot.

He lifted his gaze to find Rosa staring at him in disbelief. Horror surged through him, sharp and sudden. She'd seen every second of the bone-crushing violence.

"Aiden?" Her voice broke. "How? Th-they said you were dead."

"They're working on it."

McCrae dug wire cutters from his pocket, freed Rosa from her restraints, then shoved the tool into her hands. He jabbed a finger toward a giant spool of industrial cable thirty yards away. "Move when I tell you," he said. "And stay low."

She caught his wrist before he could turn away. "You came for us."

Even then, he was slow to meet her gaze. Too many times he'd watched people flinch when they got a real look at what he was capable of. But Rosa didn't. She looked at him like a drowning woman who'd finally found shore. There was no judgment, no flinch away. She'd seen the monster in him and, God help them both, she was grateful for it.

Somehow, that terrified him more than anything.

Holbrook's men traded fire with the Russians, dragging McCrae back to the moment.

He'd already dropped three of the Onyx shooters. The last two had the Russians pinned behind the ribs of a half-built hull. When one of the Russians finally risked a look, a well-timed round cored his skull and snapped him backward out of sight.

The buyer stumbled down the pier. He tried to sprint, his legs churning as if he were running underwater. He'd made it all of twenty feet before rifle fire marched across his back, dumping him face-first onto the ground.

With Holbrook's trade partners down, the Americans swung their rifles toward McCrae just as Rosa cut the last of the kidnapped women free.

McCrae broke from cover, the AR kicking against his shoulder as he opened fire across the pier.

One merc spun away, clutching a ruined shoulder. The other dove behind the giant propeller, blind-firing through its blades.

"Go!" McCrae roared. "Head for the ramp!"

"¡Vámonos! ¡Hacia el contenedor!" Rosa urged the women forward, one arm hooked around the youngest girl, her voice steady amid the chaos. "¡Rápido, no miren atrás!"

A round clipped McCrae's shoulder, snapping him sideways. Pain detonated down his arm, hot and electric. The wounded guard was swinging wide to flank him.

McCrae reset his grip and hammered the trigger until —click, click.

Empty.

He dropped behind a concrete barrier, gunfire chewing into the stone.

The Onyx men fanned out, methodically closing in on him just as they'd done with the Russians. Rosa and the others had made it to safety behind the coil of cable, but they wouldn't get much farther if McCrae went down here.

His hand found the Glock taken from the mercs in the van. Four rounds left against trained soldiers with assault rifles.

Shit math, even for a pro like him.

McCrae drew a breath, ready to make every shot count when—

A battered van tore through the gate, its engine screaming like a banshee.

Holbrook's men snapped toward the sound as three tons of Detroit steel came howling onto the pier. One guard dove clear at the last second. The other tried to bring his rifle up. The van caught him square and launched him over the hood before skidding to a stop.

McCrae shoved to his feet as the back doors blew open.

Hank Dolan hit the concrete, his revolver roaring with enough old-school thunder to drive the last guard back on his heels. "I'd move my ass if I was you!"

McCrae called out to the girls. "Move!" he shouted. "Everyone in the van!"

Rosa pushed the youngest girl ahead of her. "¡Súbanse! ¡Rápido!"

The others scrambled in behind her, panicked cries overlapping as they clawed into the cargo bay.

McCrae pulled open the driver's door and hauled himself behind the wheel. His shoulder screamed when he yanked the gearshift into drive. "Everyone in?"

Dolan squeezed off two more shots from the wheel gun. Then he fell onto the cargo floor.

"We're good, kid! Hit it!"

McCrae buried the accelerator. The van lurched up the ramp, tires screaming. Gunfire chased them, rounds blowing out the rear windows. Safety glass exploded inward, drawing fresh screams from the girls as it rained down on them.

Chain link raked both sides of the van as they punched through the gate, metal teeth grinding paint to bare steel.

Two hard turns put them on city streets where they could finally leave the shipyard chaos behind. McCrae glanced back: the women were huddled in the cargo bay, every face tight with the same question—are we safe?

Unfortunately, McCrae had learned long ago that getaways were rarely clean, and peace of mind never came cheap. Someone always paid. Only this time, if he had his way, it would be Holbrook and Garrison footing the bill.

## TWENTY-FIVE

The working girl behind the Blue Note turned out to be an angel in a denim skirt.

She'd barely cracked the RV door before Rosa was on the steps, breathless, words tumbling over one another. Whatever she saw in Rosa's face was enough. The girl pivoted without hesitation, turning to holler something to the company sprawled across a narrow bed.

"Now hold on a minute," he said. "I didn't drive five hours to go home with blue balls."

She was already hopping into a pair of gray sweatpants. "If you want, I can call your wife so she knows I left her with some work to do."

The john muttered something foul under his breath, then shouldered past Rosa. One hand clutched at his unbuttoned jeans, keeping them from sliding off his fat ass as he lurched toward his rig and the long drive home.

Once he was gone, the girl yanked the plug on some Christmas lights strung under the RV's awning, then gave Rosa a quick little wave to let her know the coast was clear.

Rosa eased her neighbors out of the van one at a time. With one eye on the street, Dolan guided them toward the RV's narrow door. The tiny home would work as a temporary sanctuary—an hour, maybe two—but McCrae knew that was nowhere near enough.

The Commission would come looking for those responsible for torching their deal with the Russians. He had to make sure there was no one left to finger Rosa or Dolan. He also had to find Garrison before the operator could whisper his own name in the Council's ear.

He pressed his back against the RV's aluminum skin to grab a moment's rest. His shoulder throbbed. His legs trembled with the first waves of the adrenaline crash. Every muscle ached. Did he even have enough in the tank to get this done?

Rosa stepped out of the RV after settling the others inside. The last few hours had cast a shadow over her face. Her eyes appeared sunken with exhaustion. New lines were drawn tight around her mouth. Her resemblance to Maria was suddenly unmistakable.

When she started toward him, McCrae looked away, suddenly self-conscious.

He ran the carbine's action, feeling the bolt slam home. It wasn't necessary. He'd already checked it when loading the rifle with a fresh mag. It was just something to do with his hands, a little theater so Rosa wouldn't see how closely he'd been watching her.

"How are they?" he asked, nodding toward the door.

"They'll survive," Rosa said, her voice steady despite everything. "I can't let you do it."

"Do what?"

"You plan to go after them."

He drew a slow breath. "The men on your list are in the foundry just like we thought."

Rosa stepped closer. "Then we call the police."

"You know my thoughts on that."

"The FBI?"

"Because you had so much luck with ICE?" The edge in his voice was razor-sharp, but he let it stand. He couldn't soften the blow. If he was going to keep her safe, this had to be ugly.

"Don't you think they're more likely to listen once they see the shipyard?"

McCrae groaned. "Say you got someone to listen. Someone to believe you. Someone with the clout to move on Holbrook today. The Commission will have cleaned house by then."

"The Commission? Wh-what is that?"

"Combine the reach of the cartels with the brutality of MS-13. Add enough influence to guarantee people like you don't know they exist. That's who we're dealing with."

"What about Holbrook?"

"He's nothing. A mark. A wannabe who got in over his head."

Rosa went still. Her voice dropped to a whisper. "Aiden, who are you?"

Same question. Only he could no longer dodge it. He had to tell her the truth, even if he knew it would break her heart.

And his.

"You were right," he said, going for casual as he tucked a spare mag into his jacket pocket.

"Right?"

"I am one of them."

She shook her head. "Aiden, I was upset. And confused. I don't believe that."

"Even if you knew I helped them build what we're trying to tear down?"

The last of her color drained away. She searched his face for the man who'd risked everything to save her. McCrae refused to let her find him, scrubbing every trace of humanity from his expression.

"I don't believe you," she said at last.

"That's because I'm very good at what I do."

Her chin trembled, her composure continuing to slip away. She'd made it through this whole nightmare without breaking. It gutted McCrae to know he was the one who would finally make her crack. He couldn't bear to think that the tears to come would be caused by him.

But he pushed on anyway.

He had to.

"I was in the game twelve years, Delgado. Do you have any idea how many people you can hurt in that amount of time? The lives you can ruin? The children you can orphan?"

She looked up sharply. His mouth twisted into the cruelest grin he could manage.

"But you helped. Y-you wouldn't have done that unless—"

*"I didn't do it for you!"*

Resting near the van, Dolan's head came up.

"Whatever you're feeling right now, I'm not worthy of it. You were a means to an end, girl. That's it. The people working with Holbrook hurt me, so I came to Riveton looking to hurt them. I appreciate that you helped me get that done, but the truth is—if the Commission never crossed me, your situation would be very different right now."

Her eyes were welling with tears. "I don't understand."

This last part was damn near impossible to force out. "I never would have let you get away."

Rosa flinched as if he'd slapped her. She took a step back, eyes wide with revulsion. Then she turned away and started toward the girls huddled near the RV steps.

Watching her feelings for him curdle into contempt

made McCrae long for the days when the worst pain he knew was a shotgun blast to the chest.

But he quickly found relief washing in behind his pain.

There was a real chance he'd die trying to save the rest of her friends. If he left Rosa believing he was some kind of stained-glass saint, she'd spend the rest of her life fighting to avenge him with the same spirit she'd used to crusade for the people in her community. He'd seen it in her eyes back on the pier. Some people can't leave a debt like that unpaid, and he didn't want her wasting the rest of her life trying to honor a bum like him.

McCrae went back to his rifle as Dolan approached.

"You mind telling me what that was about?" the old man asked.

McCrae shook his head.

"Fair enough. It's not like we have time to spare, anyway."

"Sorry, man, but this one has to be a solo mission."

"Boy, don't think for one second—"

"Someone has to stay with them, Hank. But I do need one last favor."

Interest sparked in Dolan's eyes.

"Think you can rig up something special for me?"

"What were you thinking?"

"Well," McCrae said, "I'd like to return their van."

Dolan studied the captured vehicle—sides peppered with bullet holes, several windows blown out, front end crumpled. A mischievous grin crept across his weathered face.

"I think I can manage," he said.

"Good. But you're right. We're short on time, so—"

"I know. Get my ass moving."

Dolan pulled the last two blocks of $C_4$ from his duffel along with detonators and enough det cord to lace the interior of the van. His arthritic hands seemed to steady as muscle memory took over.

McCrae climbed into the driver's seat. The engine coughed twice before catching on the third try—rough, but alive. With luck, she still had a few more miles left under the hood.

Slumped behind the wheel, he risked a look through the ruined windshield.

Rosa was putting on a brave face for the young girls clustered around her. They leaned in, hanging on every word like they were waiting for her to deliver another miracle. To them, she was the hero—and they weren't wrong. They'd watched Rosa stare down the devil and make him blink.

McCrae could live with that version of the story. Hell, with a role model like her in their lives, maybe they still had a shot.

In the meantime, he'd do his best to keep the devil at bay.

## TWENTY-SIX

The guards at the foundry's main gate turned toward the tortured growl of an engine pushed past its limits. A van was quickly approaching in the murky dawn light.

One guard squinted through the haze. "Is that Knox?"

He saw the smoke boiling from under the hood, the spider-webbed windshield, the row of bullet holes stitched across a side panel like Morse code spelling out disaster.

"Christ!" the other exclaimed. "Looks like he's coming in hot."

He reached for his radio, but his partner caught his wrist.

The van wasn't slowing.

It was accelerating.

Fifty yards. The engine's scream climbed an octave.

Forty. Tires howled against asphalt.

Thirty. Still nothing visible through that shattered windshield.

They couldn't see the cinder block jammed on the accelerator or the bungee cords cinched tight to hold the steering wheel in place.

The van hopped a curb, twenty feet of chain link wrapping its front bumper as it crashed through the fence. The guards dove for cover, allowing the runaway vehicle to race by them before ripping through the privacy screening and burying itself in the main building with a deafening crash.

Two heartbeats of silence followed.

Then the van went up in a blast that knocked both men off their feet.

The foundry wall folded inward, a century of brick giving way to modern chemistry. Windows were blown out in sheets of glittering glass. Chemical drums tumbled end over end.

It was through a cloud of settling debris that McCrae finally emerged from concealment.

Glass crunched under his boots as he slipped through the breach, the assault rifle steady in his grip. He'd timed his approach to reach the property just as the chaos peaked.

A guard staggered from the shadows, blood trickling from burst eardrums. Even then, he swung his pistol in a controlled arc, hunting for threats through the smoke.

McCrae dropped to one knee and brought the guard into his sights.

A clean squeeze of the trigger put a bullet in his brain.

Two more figures lurched into view, wearing full hazmat suits, their only weapons the crackling cattle prods.

McCrae snapped off a round that punched through the nearer suit's faceplate, spraying its plastic shield with blood. The second guard had just enough time to strip off his gloves and grab a rifle before McCrae made quick work of him, too.

Alarms wailed as he pushed deeper into the building, emergency strobes washing everything in epileptic red. The blast had sparked a chemical fire that filled the air with oily smoke.

The migrants stood frozen among their shovels and sorting bins. Weeks of brutality had trained them to ignore hope, to keep their heads down when violence erupted. Some probably thought this was a test, another cruel game to measure obedience.

"It's fine!" McCrae shouted, chopping a hand toward the breach. "Go! Get out now!"

A few understood immediately. They dropped their tools and bolted into the night. Others stayed rooted in place, conditioned to expect punishment for any deviation from routine.

"What are you waiting for? ¡Vámonos! ¡Ahora!"

Automatic fire chewed into a nearby pillar, spraying

McCrae with concrete chips. He rolled left, tucking in behind a forklift. A quick glance across the floor was enough to catch Garrison muscling Holbrook through the smoke toward a side exit.

He finally had eyes on the men he'd come for.

McCrae snapped the AR to his shoulder, squeezing off several shots. Garrison answered with a tight volley that drove him behind a conveyor belt. By the time McCrae could look again, they'd disappeared into a maze of industrial equipment.

McCrae ejected his mag, slapped in a fresh one. He wanted to pursue, to end this now, but movement in his periphery stole his attention.

Another yellow suit burst from the smoke, cattle prod hissing blue.

McCrae dodged the wild thrust and drove his rifle stock into the soft notch where skull met spine. The guard crumpled, his prod skittering across the concrete until it bumped against the boot of a teen worker watching from a few feet away.

McCrae scooped up the prod and shoved it into the migrant's hands. "Use it if you have to."

Something shifted in the boy's eyes—fear giving way to a flicker of possibility.

The same transformation was taking hold all around them. One man hefted a pipe wrench, his scarred hands gripping it like a weapon he finally had permission to swing. Another found a length of rebar. A third tested the weight of a shovel.

McCrae watched their focus snap to the last few guards still on their feet.

No more keeping their heads down. No more swallowing orders. No more biding their time.

The armed migrants surged toward the exit in a furious wave. Their makeshift weapons cracked knees, smashed ribs, and shattered faceplates. Yellow suits folded. Men went down screaming, trampled under boots that didn't slow on their way to freedom.

McCrae steered the kid into the stream of fleeing workers, watching him vanish in the crush. Then he slipped back into the smoke and shadows, rifle up and pulse steady, ready to finish his hunt for the two men who'd turned the foundry into a twisted version of hell on Earth.

## TWENTY-SEVEN

Sirens wailed in the distance as McCrae tracked Holbrook and Garrison to a gutted office building across the street. He'd climbed several flights when angry voices bled down from above.

"You don't even realize you've fucked us both!" Garrison shouted.

"O-okay," Holbrook stammered. "But we can't just run."

"Do whatever you want. But you're going to make this transfer first."

Four flights up, McCrae followed his rifle's barrel out onto the raw floor.

Holbrook and Garrison stood near a bank of filthy windows. Dawn light seeped through the grimy glass, washing everything in a tired gray. The waterfront sprawled below, the foundry belching black smoke.

McCrae arrived just in time to see Garrison shove an open laptop into the developer's hands.

"Fine," Holbrook said. "Just tell me how much you need."

Garrison looked like a man who was only now discovering the depths of his partner's stupidity. "The Council is going to hold me accountable for this shit. I'm going to spend the rest of my life on the run because you wanted to play gangster. I'm taking it all."

Holbrook jerked his head up from the screen. "You can't leave me with nothing."

"You'll be lucky if I leave you with your life. Now log in to your fucking account."

Holbrook just stared, frozen, wide-eyed, and sweating.

"Don't let him scare you," McCrae said. "You've still got options."

Both men spun to find McCrae standing with the AR shouldered, sight line steady, finger resting on the trigger.

"Couples therapy might work—or I can just put you both out of your misery right now."

The noise that came out of Garrison was raw and uncontrolled. His arm snapped around Holbrook's throat as his Glock came up. A moment of hesitation cost McCrae his advantage. By the time his sights caught up, Garrison had already turned Holbrook into a human shield.

McCrae slid away, dropping behind a stack of cement bags as Garrison opened fire.

The operator dragged Holbrook across the floor. It wasn't until he found cover behind a concrete pillar that he finally shoved him aside.

The entire floor was a maze of unrealized ambition. Power tools lay abandoned on the bare subfloor. Exposed rebar jutted from half-poured columns. The walls were a skeleton of steel studs and open air. Through those naked ribs, McCrae watched Holbrook crawl toward an open elevator shaft where cables dangled in the dark.

The amateur was finally out of harm's way so the professionals could go to work.

Garrison broke from cover, firing rounds as he searched for a better position.

McCrae's world narrowed to geometry and physics—angles of cover, lines of sight, trajectories of death.

He pushed to his feet, rifle tight to his shoulder when he let it roar.

A window blew out in a spray of glass. Rounds sparked off ductwork and twisted metal.

Garrison moved from column to column, never offering McCrae a clean shot.

Then—click, click, click.

The rifle ran dry.

"Shit."

Good thing Garrison's Glock was already locked back on an empty chamber.

Both men stepped into the open at once, each

studying the other through a thin cloud of concrete dust. Garrison let his pistol drop. McCrae tossed his rifle.

Experience had taught them what came next.

Garrison circled, hands loose, weight centered. "I should probably thank you."

"Why's that?" McCrae asked.

"Delivering your head to the Council might be the one thing that saves me."

McCrae could read violence in a man's shoulders. There was no bluster in Garrison, no street-tough swagger—just the promise of a clean, professional kill.

"Don't worry," Garrison said. "Out of respect, I'll make this quick."

McCrae bared his teeth. "I won't."

Garrison's jab snapped McCrae's head sideways. A hook crashed into his ribs, driving the air from his lungs. A low kick deadened the muscle of his thigh.

Each shot was sharp, economical, designed for maximum damage. Textbook work.

Unfortunately for Garrison, it was a textbook McCrae knew well.

Garrison loaded up for another combination, smooth and confident. This time McCrae slipped inside the arc. His forehead met the bridge of Garrison's nose with a wet crunch.

McCrae buried a knee in his gut, folding him over, then heaved him across a table saw. When his hip hit the switch, the power tool came to life unexpectedly, announcing itself with a high-pitched whine as its blade began to spin.

Garrison bounced back with a length of rebar in his fist. His swinging attack whistled through the air close enough to part McCrae's hair.

McCrae scrambled back, his heel catching on a loop of air hose. He staggered, nearly going down as the rebar descended in a killing arc. He caught it between his hands, but the impact drove a surge of white-hot agony into his wounded shoulder.

They slammed together around the rebar, wrestling for position, McCrae's boots skidding across the dusty floor as Garrison used raw strength to force him into the corner.

Garrison twisted the bar's angle, shifting so his full weight was behind it.

The rough steel shredded McCrae's hands as it tore through his grip.

An inch. Another. The jagged tip crept toward the hollow of McCrae's throat. In another second, the rebar would punch straight through his windpipe.

McCrae drew a breath, then drove a knee into Garrison's groin. The operator's grip went slack. McCrae wrenched the rebar free and buried it in Garrison's knee at the perfect angle.

The joint bent sideways with a sickening pop.

Garrison dropped but didn't scream. Even crippled,

he moved purposefully, dragging himself toward a pneumatic nail gun.

McCrae waited until his hand brushed the would-be weapon, then brought the bar down and shattered half the bones in Garrison's hand.

This finally ripped a primal cry from somewhere deep within him.

McCrae followed the bone-shattering attack with a right cross that broke Garrison's nose. Then he kicked the nail gun away.

The operator cradled the ruined hand against his chest. His face had gone pale beneath the blood streaming from his nose, but his eyes had come alive with hate.

"You should have stayed gone," he wheezed. "They'll never forgive this."

"It's not forgiveness I'm after," McCrae muttered.

Garrison's good hand inched toward the backup piece on his ankle. McCrae gave him just enough time to clear the leather, to feel a little hope.

Then he drove the steel bar through Garrison's throat.

His body convulsed, hands clawing at the rough metal jutting from his neck. Blood fountained around the wound, pooling on the plywood beneath him, seeping through gaps in the subfloor. His legs kicked in a violent spasm, then his whole body went still.

McCrae stood over Garrison in silence, letting the tension bleed out of him until only his bone-deep exhaustion remained.

"Jesus Christ."

Startled, he spun to find Holbrook slowly approaching.

"You killed him. I can't believe you actually..."

Favoring one leg, McCrae started toward him.

"Wait," Holbrook said, his voice rising as he backed away. "Stop! We can work this out."

"Not likely."

"You think I wanted this?! You said it yourself: the Commission forced my hand. And they burned us both, right? I'm sure the last thing they want is us working together."

McCrae slowed, saying nothing.

"By this time tomorrow, I will have told my story to every news show that matters. That alone will knock them down a peg or two. But if we can pair my influence with your... skill set... that may be enough to take them down for good."

Holbrook's vision was going up in flames, but men like him had a funny way of crawling out of the ashes with a new story and clean hands.

A dangerous thought slid into McCrae's mind before he could slam the door on it. Maybe Dean Holbrook would make a better partner than the Judge. He wasn't so different from McCrae, after all. The Commission had sunk its hooks into Holbrook the same way it had with him. Maybe the developer had spent that time wrestling with his conscience, too.

Holbrook stepped closer, fussing with a shirt cuff like he was already back in the boardroom. "Do you understand what I'm offering? It's more than a seat at my side. It's a chance to get your old life back. Only this time, you're getting in on the ground floor."

"The ground floor?"

Holbrook's smile twisted into something as dark as the poisoned smoke boiling up from the foundry. "Someone will have to fill the void when the Commission's gone."

Heat filled McCrae's chest, rage blooming fast and hot.

Holbrook's hope was snuffed out as McCrae closed the distance between them. "Wait!"

McCrae's hand clamped around Holbrook's throat, bone and tendon grinding under his grip as he drove the developer backward toward the open elevator shaft.

Holbrook's heels scraped uselessly across the dusty floor. One brutal shove carried him through the open doors, leaving only his toes on solid ground.

Four stories of nothing waited beneath him, cables swaying in the dark.

His face went from red to purple. His eyes bulged.

And in those eyes, McCrae saw them. All of them. Not just the Commission. He saw every predator who'd built an empire on the backs of those less fortunate, men living their best lives in penthouse apartments and private villas while their victims suffered in alleys all around the world.

He pictured Holbrook in Lambert's courtroom: the tailored suit, the scripted remorse, the inevitable acquittal that would follow, as it always did for men like him. He would be another shark slipping the net. The system would fail. That's why the judge didn't hire a PI.

Whether she knew it or not, she was after more than evidence.

She was searching for a better way.

McCrae opened his hand.

Holbrook's scream lasted three seconds.

The wet crash that followed seemed to go on forever.

McCrae stood at the shaft's edge, staring into the dark. Somewhere below lay a man who had enslaved dozens, murdered witnesses, and traded children like cargo.

Was this justice?

No, he would never call it that.

But he'd made sure Dean Holbrook could hurt no one again.

For now, that was enough.

## TWENTY-EIGHT

Sunlight filtered through the cramped bathroom's tiny window, soft and forgiving after the foundry fires. McCrae sat rigidly on the closed toilet seat while Rosa knelt before him, carefully cleaning the bullet graze along his shoulder.

"Hold still," she whispered, dabbing antiseptic on the wound. "This might sting."

The shoebox of first-aid supplies looked like something lifted from a family with young kids—superhero Band-Aids, children's Tylenol, calamine lotion.

An hour ago, he'd been dropping bodies. Thirty minutes ago, he'd executed an unarmed man. Now he sat in Rosa Delgado's bathroom getting patched up like a boy with a skinned knee. It was the type of care he'd prayed for as a child but never received.

If only he could find some way to make the moment last.

Rosa taped down the edges of a bandage she'd pressed over the wound. "There," she said. "It isn't perfect, but that should hold."

McCrae tested his shoulder. It was stiff but functional. "It's good. Thank you."

Rosa answered with a sad smile. "Of course."

She was packing up her collection of first-aid supplies when McCrae pulled the burner from his pocket and offered it to her.

"What's that?"

"Footage from inside the foundry."

Rosa opened one of the two videos saved on the phone. Her face paled as the images played—emaciated men handling toxic waste, guards with cattle prods, shipping containers packed with human beings forced to live in unthinkable conditions.

"I've deleted every contact but one: Blair Whitmore. She's an investigative journalist out of Chicago, but I'm told she has national reach. She'll make sure this story doesn't go away. Tell her as much or as little as you like. I don't care. All I ask is that you leave my name out of it."

While reluctant, she answered with a nod.

McCrae snagged his shirt from the counter. Pain flared as he lifted his arm to work it through the sleeve. When Rosa stepped in to help, he didn't have the energy to protest.

He watched her hands move deliberately from button to button down his chest. She seemed to make a point of going slow, stretching the seconds just like him.

They were both smart enough to know they'd never see each other again.

"You think you'll go back to school?" The question came out rougher than he'd intended.

"Once the timing's right."

"Don't put it off. Time has a funny way of speeding up on you."

She brushed loose hair from her face, eyes settling on him with a new resolve. "About those things you said—"

"I was only trying to keep you safe."

"You're nothing like them, Aiden."

The bathroom suddenly felt smaller than any cell. He had to get out, had to get back on the road to Stateville.

"I don't know who put those things in your head—but you *are* worthy."

He worried she would see the weakness he was fighting so hard to bury. "If you knew the things I've done, I'm not sure you'd say that."

"We're all outrunning something."

"Not like this."

"That might be true. But I think there's something you should consider."

"What's that?" he asked.

"What if going through that was the only way you could help us through this?"

Rosa left him with that, slipping out as if she knew it was a question he'd have to sit with for a long time before answering—if it was a question that could ever be answered.

When he finally followed her into the kitchen, McCrae found Dolan hunched over the table, shoveling scrambled eggs and black beans into his mouth. Rosa pressed a mug into his palm. The coffee was cheap but strong, exactly what he needed to keep him upright for his trip back after everything that had happened.

As he downed the cup, he let the kitchen wrap him in its embrace: crayon drawings under refrigerator magnets, a mismatched collection of chipped dishes in the sink, the soft hiss of peppers and onions simmering in a pan.

Then he saw it—a corner of glossy paper jutting from beneath a mound of junk mail.

Green. Gold. Pristine.

He slid the flyer free. RIVETON WILL RISE blazed across the top in bold letters. Beneath that, renderings of glass-faced buildings and manicured parks along the resurrected waterfront.

Holbrook's dream. Now just as dead as Holbrook.

But McCrae had done more than put a bullet in the vision of one man. He'd ruined an operation that would have funneled millions to the Commission. If only he could be there when the news reached the Council in their perch above the city.

"Do you have a marker?" McCrae asked. "A Sharpie or something like that. And an envelope."

Rosa and Dolan exchanged confused looks but kept any questions to themselves. Rosa rummaged through a drawer and returned with both items.

McCrae smoothed the flyer flat. The Sharpie squeaked as he carved a message across the paper in hard, deliberate strokes. Once finished, he folded the sheet and slid it into the envelope. He was just shoving it into his pocket when Maria shuffled excitedly into the room.

"Mamá?" Rosa said with a hint of alarm. "¿Todo bien?"

The old woman went straight for McCrae, her small hands surprisingly strong as she pulled him into the front room and through the front door.

She stopped just shy of the porch steps, turning to watch his face.

The sunbathed neighborhood had completely transformed.

Just hours ago, Holbrook's raid had turned the block into a war zone—splintered doors, shattered glass, families ripped apart.

Now many of those same families were spilling into the street, crashing into the arms of loved ones who'd had the strength to forgo the hospital and start home on foot.

A man in tattered work clothes lifted his laughing daughter onto his shoulders and spun her in a clumsy circle. A middle-aged woman squeezed her frail husband against her chest tightly enough to crack ribs. Others sank to their knees in the street, whispering prayers that the next person to come around the corner would be theirs.

McCrae's throat tightened as Rosa and Dolan stepped out to join them, the quiet weight of their presence settling at his back.

Two doors down, a sickly man with forearms etched in fresh chemical burns spotted him. The man drew himself up, shoulders squaring despite the pain.

Then he raised a fist to his chest.

Others followed. One by one, up and down the block, the survivors turned toward McCrae. Mothers with red-rimmed eyes. Fathers in coveralls eaten away by toxins.

Each of them lifted a fist and pressed it to their heart.

No cheers. No speeches. Just a silent salute, the only language big enough for a gratitude they'd never be able to voice.

The attention made McCrae feel like a fraud. He was no hero. Hell, for most of his life, he'd been a weapon waiting to serve at the pleasure of terrible men. But what if? What if all those years *had* prepared him to do something more?

Maria rose onto her toes and kissed his cheek. Her lips were rose-petal soft against his skin. She whispered something in Spanish—too fast for him to catch every word, but the blessing landed all the same.

Prison waited. Stateville's concrete and steel. Lambert's cool eyes. She would never trust him with something like this again. And the Commission? When they learned what had happened in Riveton, they would send someone to sift through the ashes.

Eventually, McCrae would have to answer for everything.

But not yet.

He knew there was nothing he could do to wash the blood from his ledger. Some debts ran too deep to ever be paid. But he was learning something far more important.

Even a weapon forged in darkness could bring some light into this world.

## TWENTY-NINE

The room hadn't changed in a week—same concrete walls, same table bolted to the floor, same fluorescents washing everything in prison green.

Only this time, Judge Lambert was already waiting for McCrae.

Her fingers tapped a steady rhythm across her laptop's keyboard. She didn't look up when the guards brought him in. Even after the door clanged shut and left him alone with her, she continued typing like he wasn't there, leaving McCrae to stand there awkwardly like some troublesome kid who'd been called to the principal's office.

He let it go, giving her a few more moments to pretend she was in control.

"Have a seat," she said at last.

He dropped into the chair across from her. When she

finally looked up, her expression softened with concern after seeing the week's violence mapped across his face.

"You should see the other guy," McCrae said with a smirk.

Her empathy was gone as quickly as it had appeared. "I have."

She spun the laptop toward him. CNN's homepage screamed INDUSTRIAL ACCIDENT IN CHICAGO SUBURBS. A photo featured pillars of black smoke twisting over Riveton's waterfront while fire crews battled the blaze.

"I sent you to observe and report, not wage war."

"I did what you wanted. If your journalist friend isn't reviewing the evidence yet—"

She stood, her chair legs scraping against the tile. "What I wanted?! Do you have any idea how many agencies are already on the ground to investigate this mess? FBI, EPA, ATF—"

"They're throwing all the letters at it, huh?"

"You're not as cute as you think. I told you to keep a low profile. I said you weren't to intervene under any circumstances. But what did you do?"

"You also called me a man who can't turn a blind eye."

"So you assumed I would turn a blind eye when you left a dozen bodies in your wake?"

He rose so she was no longer looming over him. "What did you expect me to do?"

"Exactly what we discussed. Let the evidence become

part of the public discourse. That way, the proper authorities could—"

"We're here because you lost faith in the system. I don't buy for one second that you've risked it all to build a case for some DA you know is on the take."

Her gaze slid to the laptop, to flames consuming Riveton's foundry. "This was a mistake," she said, more to herself than to him. "I don't know what I was thinking."

"Sure you do."

"Excuse me?"

"This will get a whole lot easier when you admit that I'm right."

"Right about what?"

"You didn't pick me despite my violent past. You picked me because of it."

She glared at him across the table, the silence stretching until her tough-as-nails exterior cracked just enough for McCrae to glimpse what lived beneath all that righteousness.

Lambert was as lost in the gray between right and wrong as he was.

When she spoke again, the edge was gone. "Maybe you're right," she said. "The man you saw. This Garrison. Is he—"

"He won't be telling anyone I had a hand in this."

A sound slipped out of her before she could catch it—part sigh, part gasp.

The implication was unmistakable. Garrison was

dead. And he was only dead because she'd let McCrae out of his cage.

A lot of people had died because of the plan she'd set in motion.

"That doesn't mean the Commission won't be a problem," McCrae said. "They won't just lay down. You're risking more than your career. If we move forward, every person we involve will become a target. And if they trace this back to you, every person you've ever loved."

She lifted her chin. Her spine straightened. "If we move forward?"

He answered with a nod. "But if we're doing it—we're *doing* it."

She sat with this for a long moment before finally moving to pull up a new file on her laptop. "There's something I want to show you. What do you know about pain management centers?"

McCrae needed a second to shift gears. "I suppose they're great in theory. But you can count me as a guy who thinks most are probably doing more harm than good."

Lambert's look urged him to go a little deeper.

"The Commission loves them," he said. "They lean on providers to write junk scripts, demand that they push pills to anyone through the door. And once they're hooked—"

"The Commission has dealers waiting on every corner."

"Exactly."

"Did you know they've opened several in Castle Heights?"

His hand clenched into a fist. Castle Heights—his old neighborhood. Every corner held memories. Some good, many bad. He remembered it as the place where he'd last had the courage to dream big. It was also in Castle Heights that his demons drew their first breaths.

She turned the laptop toward him, this time sharing an article about the third center to open in Castle Heights. Bright signs promised PAIN RELIEF and SAME DAY APPOINTMENTS. It was the kind of place desperate people crawled to when real doctors were too far or too expensive.

"Drug-related crime is up twenty-eight percent," Lambert explained. "Overdoses have doubled. If we're going to continue, this is where we hit them next. Once you've had time to visit the infirmary and recover from your trip to Riveton, of course."

Years had passed since he'd last set foot on his old block. He wondered how different it would look now that the Commission was hollowing it out to pad its vault with a few more stacks. Mostly, he wondered how close these new clinics were to his mother's apartment. His mother, with her weak knees, aching back, and lifelong devotion to the path of least resistance.

"Don't worry about me," he said. "You just set it up as soon as you can."

He crossed the room, rapping on the door so the guards knew he was ready to go.

Now alone, Lambert let the laptop close, something in her posture collapsing with it. Not from fatigue. This was more than the tired bones of a woman McCrae suspected was dealing with an illness. Planning their next move like this was an admission she was okay with everything he'd done over the last few days.

It was an admission that had likely cost her something she would never get back.

"I wish you could've been there," McCrae said.

Her head snapped up. "Where?"

"In Riveton. If you'd met the people we helped, you'd know it was worth the risk."

A weary smile found her. "I hope you're right."

"Have a good night, Your Honor. Be careful going home."

The door opened. He stepped into the hall and was gone before he could hear her answer.

"You too, Mr. McCrae."

# EPILOGUE

The Westlake's twenty-seventh floor offered a postcard view of the city—Lake Michigan endless to the horizon, Chicago's skyline knifing up from the shore. Many joked they would kill for the chance to go home to such a breathtaking view of the city.

Very few understood this was exactly how the Council secured it.

Jade Milano stood a few feet from the glass, hands clasped behind her back, watching the city's reflection shimmer over the lake. A wall-mounted television illuminated the room as a fresh-faced woman shared stories of human trafficking and slave labor in America's heartland. The chyron read: BLAIR WHITMORE – INVESTIGATIVE JOURNALIST / PODCASTER.

"...you're talking about the Commission," the anchor prompted, his voice pitched with manufactured shock.

Hearing the organization's name spoken that plainly on national TV elicited a low groan from the men around the table. Leather creaked as someone shifted uncomfortably in their seat. Ice clinked softly in a glass as someone took a much-needed drink.

Rather than turn, Milano studied Whitmore's reflection in the glass. Younger than she'd expected—mid-twenties, maybe. Smart eyes. Ambitious. A little too eager. Had she even taken a moment to consider the dangers waiting in this new world she was entering?

Apparently not. She was performing like this was her audition for an anchor desk.

*Stupid bitch.*

"For decades," Whitmore said, "the Commission has operated in relative anonymity while infiltrating small towns across the Midwest. But today, not only have my sources linked the Commission to last week's heinous discovery in Riveton, they've also provided us with a glimpse behind the curtain."

The screen cut to shaky phone footage: migrants in tattered clothes digging through oily waste while figures in hazmat suits loomed over them with cattle prods; men held captive in slave ship conditions, surrounded by filth, their skin cratered and gray.

Behind Milano, members of the Council murmured with increasing frustration. Riveton had been running like a well-oiled machine. Millions in potential revenue. A compliant frontman in Dean Holbrook. All of it now up in smoke.

Milano wasn't surprised. It wasn't long ago Garrison had been nothing more than a booster out of Milwaukee. She never understood why the Council thought he was the one to manage something so important—not when she was available.

The television went black with a soft click.

Rourke set the remote down, nudging it across the table as if it were contaminated. "She's been making the rounds all day. CNN, Fox. My wife saw her pulling this shit on *The View*."

Two seats down, Berg scrolled on his phone. "The podcast had close to one hundred thousand downloads in the first twenty-four hours."

Kellerman's nephew finally pulled his feet off the table. Sneakers, for Christ's sake. "I'll just say it: every minute this bitch spends on this side of the dirt is a mistake."

"You don't kill someone when they have the world's attention," Kellerman said from his spot near the head of the table.

"So we just let her run her mouth to anyone who'll listen?"

"For now. But when the spotlight's gone, we'll sit her down for an interview she won't forget."

"She's not the one to worry about," Milano said matter-of-factly.

Everyone turned as if they'd forgotten she was there.

"I'm more concerned with the person who put that footage in her hands."

Evan scoffed. "Probably some random illegal with a phone up his ass."

Milano slowly cut her gaze toward the kid. "You think it was some random immigrant who took down an Onyx Shield security team? Who put a piece of steel through Garrison's neck?"

Evan looked ready to shoot off at the mouth but thought better of it.

Maybe the nepobaby was smarter than everyone thought.

Milano's focus shifted to the other men at the table. Rourke with his perfect knot and polished aggression. Berg hunched over numbers. Kellerman at the head, older now, his power sitting on him like an ill-fitting coat.

"This wasn't random," she said. "It feels more like an attack."

Before anyone could respond, the suite door eased open.

A young woman in a Westlake uniform appeared in the doorway. Strangely, she was clutching a folded slip of paper like she worried it might go off in her hand. "I'm sorry to interrupt, but this seemed… important."

"Can't you see we're in the middle of something?" Evan snapped.

"Easy," Kellerman said softly.

Rourke turned on the charm. "Just leave it, sweetheart. We'll get to it when we can."

She hovered, searching for a place to set the letter that wouldn't require her to step farther into the room.

Evan shoved his chair back with a loud scrape. "Jesus. It's not that hard."

He was on her in a flash, fingers clamping around her arm. She gasped, the paper slipping from her hand as he spun her toward the hall. He pushed the door into her, using its weight to shove her out faster, knocking her off balance as it closed behind her.

"Was that necessary?" Rourke asked.

"I'm not the one screwing her."

Milano noticed a flicker of displeasure on Rourke's face. Good. She wasn't the only one sick of the kid's obnoxious act. When the time came, Rourke might be an ally.

"Uncle Francis?" Something at Evan's feet put a tremor in his voice. He bent, scooped up the glossy flyer, then handed it to his uncle.

Green. Gold. Pristine.

Kellerman's face fell. He slid the flyer across the table for the others to see. It featured an architect's rendering of glass towers and manicured walkways along a resurrected waterfront. Across the top, a slogan was printed in bold letters: RIVETON WILL RISE.

Only someone had drawn a violent X through the text. Beneath it, in block letters carved with conviction, someone had written their own message: THE COMMISSION WILL FALL.

The table erupted as every member of the Council suddenly fought to be heard. Milano was content to let their panic bloom without adding her voice.

Her thoughts turned to the crime scene photos passed along by their inside man. Garrison on his back, the concrete around him black with arterial spray. The bodies of Onyx men scattered across the shipyard. Riveton's old mill blown off the map, nothing left behind but twisted steel and fire.

The official story was that the enslaved migrants had staged an uprising.

Bullshit.

This was the work of a professional. More than that, the violence felt personal. Now, this flyer confirmed it. After years of preying on the weakest links in the food chain, the Commission had finally crossed someone willing to make these predators his prey. Someone with the balls to sign his work.

And it was only the beginning.

Milano grinned. This would be her masterpiece. Hunting down this new adversary would finally force the Council to admit what she'd known for years: that the open seat among them belonged to her. If not, they'd only have themselves to blame when she took it all.

## STATEVILLE CORRECTIONAL
### INMATE CORRESPONDENCE

I told Lambert you'd only get in my way.

Turns out, I was wrong.

If you're game to keep putting heat on the Commission, there's just one way to get word to me while I'm on the inside—that's Amazon.

Five stars. A few lines about why you're not finished.

Do that. I'll handle the rest.

   -McCrae

## STAY IN THE SHADOWS

McCrae's war with the Commission is just getting started.

**Join the E.S. Hobbs mailing list** for access to:

→ BTS details as books came together—the research, the late nights, the scenes that hit the cutting room floor

→ Early word on new books before others know they exist

→ Special offers available nowhere else

No spam. No noise. Just the good stuff, when it matters.

**Sign up at: eshobbs.com/join**

The Council thinks they're untouchable.

Let's prove them wrong.

-E.S. Hobbs

Aiden McCrae returns to Castle Heights—where his childhood home still stands, his mother still lives, and the Commission deals death by prescription.

Pain management clinics are spreading across the Rust Belt, turning desperate patients into addicts—and addicts into corpses. The pill mill operation is raking in millions for his former employers. To shut it down, McCrae must confront a past he'd rather forget—and the family who broke him long before the Commission could.

When the war comes home, the past fights back.

**Preorder PAIN TRADE today.**

# ABOUT THE AUTHOR

E.S. Hobbs writes crime thrillers set in the overlooked neighborhoods of the Midwest—places littered with rusted-out mills, seedy motels, and streets where desperation pushes ordinary people to do terrible things. *Grave Cargo* is his debut thriller.

Printed in Dunstable, United Kingdom